Pollyanna

by ELEANOR H. PORTER

Abridged and Edited
by Molly Harrington

Cover illustration by John Fernie

SCHOLASTIC BOOK SERVICES
NEW YORK•TORONTO•LONDON•AUCKLAND•SYDNEY•TOKYO

Copyright 1912, 1913, and Renewed 1940, 1941 by L.C. Page and Company (now Farrar, Straus & Giroux, Inc.). This abridged version Copyright © 1975 by Farrar, Straus & Giroux, Inc. This edition is published by Scholastic Book Services, a division of Scholastic Magazines, Inc., by arrangement wth Farrar, Straus & Giroux, Inc.

14 13 12 11 10 9 8 7 6 5 4 3   7 8 9/7 01/8

Printed in the U.S.A.

Contents

Miss Polly

MISS POLLY HARRINGTON entered her kitchen a little hurriedly. Miss Polly did not usually make hurried movements, but this June morning she was hurrying — actually hurrying.

Nancy, washing dishes at the sink, looked up in surprise. Nancy had been working in Miss Polly's kitchen for only two months, but already she knew that her mistress did not usually hurry.

"Nancy!"

"Yes, ma'am." Nancy answered cheerfully as she continued wiping the pitcher in her hand.

"Nancy." Miss Polly's voice was very stern now. "When I'm talking to you, I wish you

1

to stop your work and listen to what I have to say."

Nancy set the pitcher down at once with the cloth still about it, thereby nearly tipping it over.

"Yes, ma'am. I will, ma'am," Nancy stammered. "I was only keeping on with my work 'cause you specially told me this morning to hurry with my dishes, you know."

"That will do, Nancy. I did not ask for explanations. I asked for your attention."

"Yes, ma'am." Nancy stifled a sigh. She was wondering if she could ever please this woman. Nancy had never "worked out" before, but when her sick mother had been suddenly widowed and left with three younger children besides Nancy, the girl had been forced into doing something toward their support. She had been so pleased when she found a place in the kitchen of the great house on the hill. She came from "The Corners," six miles away, and she knew Miss Polly Harrington only as the mistress of the old Harrington homestead, and one of the wealthiest residents of the town. That was two months before. She knew Miss Polly now as a stern, severe-faced woman who frowned if a knife clattered to the floor or if a door banged.

"When you've finished your morning work,

Nancy," Miss Polly was saying now, "you may clear the little room at the head of the stairs in the attic, and make up the cot bed. Sweep the room and clean it, of course, after you clear out the trunks and boxes."

"Yes, ma'am. And where shall I put the things that I take out?"

"In the front attic." Miss Polly hesitated, then went on. "I suppose I may as well tell you now, Nancy. My niece, Miss Pollyanna Whittier, is coming to live with me. She is eleven years old, and will sleep in that room."

"A little girl — coming here, Miss Harrington? Oh, won't that be nice!" cried Nancy.

"That isn't exactly the word I should use," answered Miss Polly. "However, I intend to make the best of it. I am a good woman and I hope I know my duty."

Nancy colored hotly.

"Of course, ma'am. It was only that I thought a little girl might — might brighten things up for you," she faltered.

"Thank you," rejoined the lady dryly. "I can't say that I see any need for that, however."

"But of course you'd want your sister's child," ventured Nancy.

Miss Polly lifted her chin haughtily.

"Really, Nancy, just because I happened

to have a sister, who was silly enough to marry and bring unnecessary children into a world that was already quite full enough, is no reason why I should particularly want to have the care of them. However, as I said before, I hope I know my duty. See that you clean the corners, Nancy," she finished sharply, as she left the room.

"Yes, ma'am," sighed Nancy, picking up the half-dried pitcher.

In her own room, Miss Polly took out the letter which she had received two days before and which had been so unpleasant a surprise to her. The letter, from a small town in the West, was addressed to Miss Polly Harrington, Beldingsville, Vermont, and it read as follows:

"DEAR MADAM: — I regret to inform you that the Rev. John Whittier died two weeks ago, leaving one child, a girl eleven years old. He left practically nothing else save a few books, for, as you doubtless know, he was the pastor of this small mission church and had a very meager salary.

"I believe he was your deceased sister's husband, but he gave me to understand the families were not on the best of terms. He thought, however, that for your sister's sake you might wish to take the child and bring her up among her own people in the East. Hence, I am writing to you.

"The little girl will be all ready to start by the time you get this letter. If you can take her, we would appreciate it very much if you would write that she might come at once as there is a man and his wife here who are going East very soon. They would take her with them to Boston, and put her on the Beldingsville train. Of course you would be notified what day and train to expect Pollyanna on.

"Hoping to hear favorably from you soon, I remain,

"Respectfully yours,
"JEREMIAH O. WHITE."

With a frown Miss Polly folded the letter and tucked it into its envelope. She had answered it the day before, and she had said she would take the child. She hoped she knew her duty well enough for that! — disagreeable as the task would be.

As she sat now with the letter in her hands, her thoughts went back to her sister Jennie and to the time when Jennie, as a girl of twenty, had insisted upon marrying the young minister.

There had been a man of wealth who had wanted to marry Jennie, and her family had preferred him to the minister, but Jennie had not. The minister had only a young head full of ideas and enthusiasm, and a heart full of love. Jennie had preferred these to money, so she had married the minister and had gone away with him as a home missionary's wife.

The break had come then. Miss Polly remembered it well, though she had been only a girl of fifteen at the time. The family had had little more to do with the missionary's wife. To be sure Jennie had written for a time, and had named her last baby "Pollyanna" for her two sisters, Polly and Anna — her other babies had all died. This had been the last time that Jennie had written. In a few years the news of her death had come in a short, heartbroken note from the minister himself.

Meanwhile, time had not stood still for the occupants of the great house on the hill. Miss Polly, looking out at the far-reaching valley below, thought of the changes those twenty-five years had brought to her.

She was forty now, and quite alone in the world. Father, mother, sisters — all were dead. For years now she had been sole mistress of the house and of the thousands left her by her father. There were people who had openly pitied her and who had urged her to have some friend or companion to live with her, but she had not welcomed either their sympathy or their advice. She was not lonely, she said. She liked being by herself. She preferred quiet. But now —

Miss Polly rose with a frowning face and closely shut lips. She was glad, of course, that she was a good woman, and that she not only knew her duty but had sufficient strength of character to perform it. But — *Pollyanna!* — what a ridiculous name!

Old Tom and Nancy

IN THE LITTLE ATTIC ROOM Nancy swept and scrubbed vigorously, paying particular attention to the corners.

"I — just — wish — I could — dig — out — the corners — of — her — soul!" she muttered, punctuating her words with murderous jabs of her pointed cleaning stick. "Unnecessary children, indeed! Humph!" snapped Nancy, wringing her rag so hard her fingers ached from the strain.

For some time she worked in silence. Then, her task finished, she looked about the bare little room in plain disgust.

"Well, it's done — my part, anyhow," she

said. "There ain't no dirt here, and there's mighty little else. Poor little soul! A pretty place this is to put a homesick, lonesome child into!" she muttered, going out and closing the door with a bang.

In the garden that afternoon, Nancy found a few minutes to talk to Old Tom, who had pulled the weeds and shoveled the paths about the place for uncounted years.

"Mr. Tom," began Nancy, throwing a quick glance over her shoulder to make sure she was unobserved. "Did you know a little girl was coming here to live with Miss Polly?"

"A what?" demanded the old man, straightening his bent back with difficulty.

"A little girl — to live with Miss Polly."

"Go on with your joking," scoffed Tom. "Why don't ye tell me the sun is a-going to set in the East tomorrow?"

"But it's true. She told me so herself," maintained Nancy. "It's her niece and she's eleven years old."

The man's jaw fell.

"So! I wonder, now," he muttered. "It ain't — but it must be — Miss Jennie's little girl! Why Nancy, it must be Miss Jennie's little girl. Glory be! to think of my old eyes a-seeing this!"

"Who was Miss Jennie?"

"She was an angel straight out of Heaven," breathed the old man. "But the old master and missus knew her as their oldest daughter. She was twenty when she married and went away from here long years ago. Her babies all died, I heard, except the last one, and that must be the one what's a-coming."

"She's eleven years old."

"Yes, she might be," nodded the old man.

"And she's going to sleep in the attic — more shame to her!" scolded Nancy, with another glance over her shoulder toward the house.

Old Tom frowned. The next moment a curious smile curved his lips.

"I'm a-wondering what Miss Polly will do with a child in the house," he said.

"Humph! Well, I'm a-wondering what a child will do with Miss Polly in the house!" snapped Nancy.

The old man grinned.

"I'm afraid you ain't fond of Miss Polly," he said.

"As if *anybody* could be fond of her!" scorned Nancy.

"I guess maybe you didn't know Miss Polly'd been in love once," he said slowly.

"Her! No! — and I guess nobody else didn't, neither."

"Oh, yes they did," nodded the old man. "And the feller's living today — right in this town too."

"Who is he?"

"I ain't a-telling that. It ain't fit that I should." The old man drew himself erect. In his dim blue eyes was pride in the family he had served and loved for long years.

"But it don't seem possible — her in love," Nancy still maintained.

Old Tom shook his head.

"You didn't know Miss Polly as I did," he argued. "She used to be real handsome — and she would be now, if she'd let herself be."

"Handsome! Miss Polly!"

"Yes. If she'd just let that hair of hers all out loose and careless-like, as it used to be, and wear dresses all lace and white — you'd see she'd be handsome! Miss Polly ain't old, Nancy."

"Ain't she, though? Well, then she's giving an awfully good imitation of it," sniffed Nancy.

"Yes, I know," Old Tom nodded. "It begun then — at the time of the trouble with her young man. It seems as if she's been feeding on wormwood an' thistles ever since — she's that bitter an' prickly to deal with."

"I should say she is," declared Nancy, indignantly. "There's no pleasing her, nohow, no matter how you try! I wouldn't stay if it wasn't for the wages and the folks at home what's needing 'em. But some day — some day I shall just boil over, and when I do it'll be good-by Nancy for me."

Old Tom shook his head.

"I know. I've felt it. It's natural — but 'tain't best, child, 'tain't best. Take my word for it, 'tain't best."

"Nancy!" called a sharp voice.

"Y-yes, ma'am," stammered Nancy, and she hurried toward the house.

The Coming of Pollyanna

IN DUE TIME the telegram came announcing that Pollyanna would arrive in Beldingsville the next day — the twenty-fifth of June — at four o'clock. Miss Polly read the telegram, frowned, then climbed the stairs to the attic room. She was still frowning as she looked about her.

The room contained a small bed, neatly made, two straight-backed chairs, a washstand, a bureau — without any mirror — and a small table. There were no curtains at the dormer windows, no pictures on the wall. All day the sun had been pouring down on the roof, and the little room was hot as an oven. As there were no screens, the windows had not been opened.

A big fly was buzzing angrily at one of them now, trying to get out.

Miss Polly killed the fly and swept it through the window, raising the sash an inch for the purpose. She straightened a chair, frowned again, and left the room.

"Nancy," she said a few minutes later at the kitchen door, "I found a fly upstairs in Miss Pollyanna's room. The window must have been raised at some time. I have ordered screens, but until they come I shall expect you to see that the windows remain closed. My niece will arrive tomorrow at four o'clock. I want you to meet her at the station. Timothy will take the open buggy and drive you over. The telegram says 'light hair, red-checked gingham dress, and straw hat.' That is all I know, but I think it is sufficient for your purpose."

"Yes, ma'am, but you — "

Miss Polly evidently read the pause right, for she frowned and said crisply:

"No, I shall not go. It is not necessary that I should, I think. That is all." And she turned away.

In the kitchen, Nancy sent her flatiron across the dishtowel she was ironing with a vicious dig.

" 'Light hair, red-checked gingham dress,

and straw hat' — all she knows indeed! Well, I'd be ashamed to own up to it, that I would."

Promptly at twenty minutes to four the next afternoon, Timothy and Nancy drove off in the open buggy. Timothy was Old Tom's son. It was sometimes said in the town that if Old Tom was Miss Polly's right-hand man, Timothy was her left.

Timothy was a good-natured youth, and a good-looking one as well. Short as Nancy's stay at the house had been, the two were already good friends. Today, however, Nancy was not her usual talkative self. She took the drive to the station almost in silence and alighted to wait for the train.

Over and over in her mind she was saying it: "Light hair, red-checked dress, straw hat."

"I hope for her sake she's quiet and sensible, and don't drop knives or bang doors," she said to Timothy, who had sauntered up to her.

"Well, if she ain't, I don't know what'll become of the rest of us," Timothy grinned. "Gorry! there goes the whistle now."

"Oh, Timothy, I — I think it was mean to send me," chattered Nancy, as she turned and hurried to a point where she could watch the passengers alight at the little station.

It was not long before Nancy saw her — a slender little girl in red-checked gingham with

15

two fat braids of flaxen hair hanging down her back. Beneath the straw hat, an eager, freckled face turned to the right and to the left, plainly searching for someone.

Nancy knew the child at once, but could not control her shaking knees sufficiently to go to her. The little girl was standing by herself when Nancy finally did approach her.

"Are you Miss — Pollyanna?" she faltered. The next moment Nancy found herself half smothered in the clasp of two gingham-clad arms.

"Oh, I'm so glad, glad, GLAD to see you," cried an eager voice in her ear. "Of course I'm Pollyanna, and I'm so glad you came to meet me! I hoped you would."

"You — you did?" stammered Nancy, wondering how Pollyanna could have known her and wanted her. "You did?" she repeated, trying to straighten her hat.

"Oh, yes and I've been wondering all the way here what you looked like," cried the little girl, dancing on her toes and sweeping the embarrassed Nancy from head to foot with her eyes. "And now I know, and I'm glad you look just like you do look."

Nancy was relieved just then to have Timothy come up. Pollyanna's words had been most confusing.

"This is Timothy. Maybe you have a trunk?" she asked.

"Yes, I have." Pollyanna nodded importantly. "I've got a brand-new one. The Ladies' Aid bought it for me. I've got a check here in my bag that Mr. Gray said I must give to you before I can get my trunk. Mr. Gray is Mrs. Gray's husband. They're cousins of Deacon Carr's wife. I came East with them, and they're lovely! Here it is," she finished, producing the check after much fumbling in the bag she carried.

Nancy drew a long breath. Then she stole a glance at Timothy, whose eyes were studiously turned away.

The three were off at last, with Pollyanna's trunk in back, and Pollyanna herself snugly ensconced between Nancy and Timothy. During the whole process of getting started, the little girl had kept up an uninterrupted stream of comments and questions. The somewhat dazed Nancy found herself quite out of breath trying to keep up with her.

"There! Isn't this lovely? Is it far? I hope it is — I love to ride," Pollyanna sighed as the wheels began to turn. "What a pretty street! I knew it was going to be pretty, Father told me — "

She stopped with a little choking breath.

Nancy, looking at her apprehensively, saw that her chin was quivering, and that her eyes were full of tears. In a moment, however, she hurried on.

"Father told me all about it. He remembered. And — I ought to have explained before. Mrs. Gray told me to, at once — about this red gingham dress, you know, and why I'm not in black. She said you'd think it was queer. But there weren't any black things in the last barrel of clothes the missionary society sent us.

"Part of the Ladies' Aid wanted to buy me a black dress and hat, but the other part thought the money ought to go toward a red carpet they're trying to get — for the church, you know."

Pollyanna paused for breath, and Nancy managed to say: "Well, I'm sure it'll be all right."

"I'm glad you feel that way." Pollyanna nodded again with that choking little breath.

"Of course, it would have been a good deal harder to be glad in black — "

"Glad!" gasped Nancy, surprised into an interruption.

"Yes — that Father's gone to Heaven to be with Mother and the rest of us. He said I must be glad. But it's been pretty hard. I didn't have anybody but the members of the Ladies' Aid

Society of the church. But now I'm sure it'll be easier because I've got you, Aunt Polly. I'm so glad I've got you!"

Nancy's sympathy for the poor little girl suddenly turned into shocked terror.

"Oh, but you've made an awful mistake, d-dear," she faltered. "I ain't your Aunt Polly!"

"You — you aren't?" stammered the little girl, in plain dismay.

"No. I'm only Nancy. I never thought of your taking me for her. We ain't a bit alike — we ain't, we ain't!"

Timothy chuckled softly, but Nancy was too disturbed to answer the merry flash from his eyes.

"But who *are* you?" questioned Pollyanna. "You don't look a bit like a Ladies' Aider!"

Timothy laughed outright this time.

"I'm Nancy, the hired girl. I do all the work except the washing an' hard ironing. Mrs. Durgin does that."

"But there is an Aunt Polly?" asked the girl, anxiously.

"You bet your life there is," cut in Timothy.

Pollyanna relaxed visibly.

"Oh, that's all right, then." There was a moment's silence, then she went on: "I'm glad that she didn't come to meet me because now

I've got her still coming, and I've got you be-sides."

"I call that a pretty slick compliment," Timothy said. "Why don't you thank the little lady?"

"I — I was thinking about Miss Polly," faltered Nancy.

Pollyanna sighed contentedly.

"I was too. You know she's all the aunt I've got, and I didn't know I had her for ever so long. Then Father told me. He said she lived in a lovely great big house way on top of a hill."

"She does. You can see it now," said Nancy. "It's that big white one with the green blinds, way ahead."

"Oh, how pretty! And what a lot of trees and grass all around it! Is my Aunt Polly rich, Nancy?"

"Yes, Miss."

"I'm so glad. It must be perfectly lovely to have lots of money. I never knew anyone that did have, only the Whites — they're some rich. They have carpets in every room and ice cream on Sundays. Does Aunt Polly have ice cream on Sundays?"

Nancy shook her head. Her lips twitched.

"No, Miss. Your aunt don't like ice cream, leastways I never saw it on her table."

Pollyanna's face fell.

"Oh, doesn't she? I'm so sorry! I don't see how she can help liking ice cream. Maybe Aunt Polly has got the carpets, though."

"Yes, she's got the carpets."

"In every room?"

"Well, in almost every room," answered Nancy, frowning suddenly at the thought of the bare little attic room where there was no carpet.

"Oh, I'm so glad," exulted Pollyanna. "I love carpets. We didn't have any, only two little rugs that came in a missionary barrel, and one of those had ink spots on it. Mrs. White had pictures too. Don't you just love pictures?"

"I — I don't know," answered Nancy in a half-stifled voice.

"I do. We didn't have any pictures. But I'm glad now we didn't have any of those nice things, 'cause I shall like Aunt Polly's all the better — not being used to 'em, you see. My, but isn't this a perfectly beautiful house!" she broke off as they turned into the wide driveway.

When Timothy was unloading the trunk, Nancy found an opportunity to mutter low in his ear:

"Don't you never say nothing to me again about leaving, Timothy Durgin. You couldn't hire me to leave!"

"Leave! I should say not," he replied. "You

couldn't drag *me* away. With that kid around, it'll be more fun here now than a moving picture show every day!"

"Fun! Fun!" repeated Nancy, indignantly. "I guess it'll be something more than fun for that blessed child when them two tries to live together. I guess she'll be a-needing some rock to fly to for refuge. Well, I'm a-going to be that rock, Timothy. I am, I am!" she vowed, as she turned and led Pollyanna up the broad steps.

The Little Attic Room

Miss Polly Harrington did not rise to meet her niece. She looked up from her book as Nancy and Pollyanna appeared in the sitting room doorway, and held out a hand with "duty" written large on every coldly extended finger.

"How do you do, Pollyanna? I — " She had no chance to say more. Pollyanna had fairly flown across the room and flung herself into her aunt's lap.

"Oh, Aunt Polly, Aunt Polly, I don't know how to be glad enough that you let me come to live with you." She was sobbing. "You don't know how perfectly lovely it is to have you and Nancy and all this after you've had just the Ladies' Aid!"

"Very likely," rejoined Miss Polly, stiffy, trying to unclasp the small, clinging fingers, and turning frowning eyes on Nancy in the doorway. "Nancy, that will do. You may go. Pollyanna, be good enough, please, to stand in a proper manner. I don't know yet what you look like."

Pollyanna drew back at once.

"No, I suppose you don't. But you see I'm not very much to look at, anyway, on account of the freckles. Oh, and I ought to explain about the red gingham. I told Nancy how Father said — "

"Yes. Well, never mind now what your father said," interrupted Miss Polly, crisply. "You had a trunk, I presume?"

"Oh, yes, indeed, Aunt Polly. I've got a beautiful trunk. I haven't got very much in it — of my own, I mean. But there were all Father's books, and Mrs. White said she thought I ought to have them. You see, Father — "

"Pollyanna," interrupted her aunt again, "there is one thing that might just as well be understood right away. I do not care to have you keep talking to me of your father."

The little girl drew in her breath.

"Why, Aunt Polly, you — you mean — "
She hesitated, and her aunt filled the pause.

"We will go upstairs to your room. Your
trunk is already there, I presume. I told Timothy to take it up — if you had one. You may
follow me, Pollyanna."

Without speaking, Pollyanna turned and followed her aunt from the room. Her eyes were
brimming with tears, but her chin was held
high.

"I'm glad she doesn't want me to talk about
Father," Pollyanna was thinking. "It'll be easier, maybe, if I don't talk about him. Probably
that is why she told me not to talk about
him." Pollyanna, convinced anew of her aunt's
"kindness," blinked off the tears.

She was on the stairway now. Just ahead,
her aunt's black silk skirt rustled luxuriously.
Behind her an open door allowed a glimpse of
soft-tinted rugs and satin-covered chairs. Beneath her feet a marvelous carpet was like
green moss to the tread. On every side the gilt
of picture frames or the glint of sunlight
through the filmy mesh of lace curtains flashed
in her eyes.

"Oh, Aunt Polly, what a perfectly lovely
house! How awfully glad you must be you're
so rich!"

"*Pollyanna!*" erupted her aunt, turning

sharply about as she reached the head of the stairs. "I'm surprised at you — making a speech like that to me!"

"Why, Aunt Polly, *aren't* you?" queried Pollyanna, in frank wonder.

"Certainly not, Pollyanna. I hope I could not forget myself so far as to be sinfully proud of any gift the Lord has seen fit to bestow upon me. Certainly not of *riches!*" declared the lady.

Miss Polly turned and walked down the hall toward the attic stairway door. She was glad now that she had put the child in the attic room. Her idea had been to get her niece as far away as possible from herself, and at the same time place her where she would not destroy valuable furnishings. Now — with this evident strain of vanity showing so early — it was all the more fortunate that the room planned for her was plain and sensible, thought Miss Polly.

Eagerly Pollyanna's feet pattered behind her aunt. Her mind turned to the wondrously exciting problem: Behind which of all these fascinating doors was her room — the dear, beautiful room, full of curtains, rugs, and pictures, that was to be her very own? Then abruptly her aunt opened a door and ascended another stairway.

A bare wall rose on either side. At the top

of the stairs, wide reaches of shadowy space
led to far corners, where the roof came down
almost to the floor and where innumerable
trunks and boxes were stacked. It was hot and
stifling. Unconsciously Pollyanna lifted her
head higher — it seemed so hard to breathe.
Then she saw that her aunt had thrown open
a door at the right.

"There, Pollyanna. Here is your room, and
your trunk is here, I see. Have you your key?"

Pollyanna nodded dumbly. Her eyes were a
little wide and frightened.

Her aunt frowned.

"When I ask a question, Pollyanna, I prefer
that you answer aloud — not merely with your
head."

"Yes, Aunt Polly."

"Thank you. That is better. I believe you
have everything that you need here," she
added, glancing at the well-filled towel rack
and water pitcher. "I will send Nancy up to
help you unpack. Supper is at six o'clock," she
finished, as she left the room and swept downstairs.

For a moment Pollyanna stood quite still.
Then she turned her wide eyes to the bare
wall, the bare floor, the bare windows. She
turned them last to the little trunk. The next
moment she stumbled blindly toward it and
fell on her knees beside it.

Nancy found her there when she came up a few minutes later.

"There, there, you poor lamb," she crooned, dropping to the floor and drawing the little girl into her arms. "I was afraid I'd find you like this. There, there, child. Come, let's have your key and we'll get inside this trunk and take out your dresses."

Somewhat tearfully Pollyanna produced the key.

"There aren't very many," she said.

"Then they're all the sooner unpacked," declared Nancy.

Pollyanna gave a sudden smile.

"That's so! I can be glad of that, can't I?"

Nancy stared.

"Why, of course," she answered a little uncertainly.

Nancy's capable hands made short work of unpacking the books, the patched undergarments, and the few pitifully unattractive dresses. Pollyanna, smiling now, flew about, hanging the dresses in the closet, stacking the books on the table, and putting away the undergarments in the bureau drawers.

"I'm sure it's going to be a very nice room. Don't you think so?" she asked after a while.

There was no answer. Nancy was very busy, apparently, with her head in the trunk. Pollyanna, standing at the bureau, gazed a little wistfully at the bare wall above.

"And I can be glad there isn't any looking glass here, 'cause where there isn't any glass I can't see my freckles."

Nancy made a sudden queer sound with her mouth, but when Pollyanna turned, her head was in the trunk again. At one of the windows, a few minutes later, Pollyanna gave a glad cry.

"Oh Nancy, I hadn't seen this before," she breathed. "Look, way off there, with those trees and the houses and that lovely church spire and the river shining just like silver. Why, Nancy, nobody needs pictures with that to look at. Oh, I'm glad now she let me have this room!"

To Pollyanna's surprise and dismay, Nancy burst into tears. Pollyanna hurriedly crossed to her side.

"Why, Nancy, Nancy, what is it?" she cried. "This wasn't your room, was it?"

"My room!" stormed Nancy, choking back the tears. "If you ain't a little angel, and if some folks don't eat dirt before — Oh land! there's her bell!" Nancy sprang to her feet, dashed out of the room, and went clattering down the stairs.

Left alone, Pollyanna went back to the window. She touched the sash tentatively. To her joy it moved under her fingers. The next moment the window was wide open, and Pollyanna was leaning far out.

A big fly swept past her nose and buzzed noisily about the room. Then another came, and another, but Pollyanna paid no heed. She had made a wonderful discovery: Against this window a huge tree flung great branches. To Pollyanna they looked like arms outstretched, inviting her.

"I believe I can do it," she said. The next moment she had climbed to the window ledge. From there it was an easy matter to step to the nearest branch. She swung herself from limb to limb until she reached the lowest branch. The drop to the ground was a little fearsome even for Pollyanna, who was used to climbing trees. She took it, however, and landed on all fours in the soft grass. Then she picked herself up and looked about eagerly.

She was at the back of the house. Before her lay a garden in which a bent old man was working. Beyond the garden a path led through an open field up a steep hill, at the top of which a lone pine tree stood on guard beside a huge rock. To Pollyanna, at the moment, there seemed to be just one place in the world worth being — on top of that big rock.

Fifteen minutes later the great clock in the

hallway of the Harrington homestead struck six. At precisely the last stroke Nancy sounded the bell for supper.

One, two, three minutes passed. Miss Polly frowned and tapped the floor with her shoe. Then she rose to her feet, went into the hall, and looked upstairs, plainly impatient. For a minute she listened intently, then she turned and swept into the dining room.

"Nancy," she said with decision, "my niece is late. No, you need not call her," she added severely as Nancy made a move toward the hall door. "I told her what time supper was, and now she will have to suffer the consequences. She may as well begin at once to learn to be punctual. When she comes down she may have bread and milk in the kitchen."

"Yes, ma'am." It was well, perhaps, that Miss Polly did not happen to be looking at Nancy's face just then.

At the earliest possible moment after supper, Nancy crept up the back stairs to the attic room.

"Bread and milk, indeed, when the poor lamb's only just cried herself to sleep," Nancy muttered fiercely as she softly pushed open the door. The next moment she gave a frightened cry. "Where are you? Where have you gone?" she cried, looking in the closet, under the bed, and even in the trunk and down the water pitcher. Then she flew downstairs and out to Old Tom in the garden.

"Mr. Tom, Mr. Tom, she's gone. She's vanished!"

The old man straightened up.

"Gone?" he repeated, unconsciously sweeping the brilliant sunset sky with his gaze. He stopped, stared for a moment intently, then turned with a slow grin. "Well, Nancy, it looks like she tried to get as nigh Heaven as she could," he said, pointing to the rock.

"If the mistress asks, tell her I ain't forgettin' the dishes, but I gone on a stroll." Nancy flung the words back over her shoulder as she sped toward the path that led through the open field.

The Game

"Miss Pollyanna, what a scare you did give me," panted Nancy, hurrying up to the big rock.

"Scare? Oh, I'm sorry. But you mustn't ever get scared about me, Nancy. Father and the Ladies' Aid used to, till they found I always come back all right."

"But I didn't even know you'd went," cried Nancy, tucking the little girl's hand under her arm and hurrying her down the hill. "I didn't see you go. Nobody did."

"I came down the tree."

Nancy stopped short.

"You did what?"

"Came down the tree outside my window."

"My stars and stockings!" gasped Nancy, hurrying on again. "I'd like to know what your aunt would say to that!"

"Would you? Well, I'll tell her, then."

"No, — no!" gasped Nancy.

"Why you don't mean she'd care!" cried Pollyanna, plainly disturbed.

"No — er — yes — well, never mind. I ain't so very particular about knowing what she'd say," stammered Nancy. "But, say, we better hurry. I've got to get them dishes done, ye know."

"I'll help," offered Pollyanna, promptly.

"Oh, Miss Pollyanna!" protested Nancy.

For a moment there was silence. The sky was darkening fast. Pollyanna shivered and took a firmer hold of her friend's arm.

"I'm glad that you did get scared — a little, 'cause you came after me."

"Poor little lamb! And, you must be hungry too. I'm afraid you'll have to have bread and milk in the kitchen with me. Your aunt didn't like it because you didn't come down to supper. I'm sorry about the bread and milk."

"Oh I'm not. I'm glad."

"Glad! Why?"

"I like bread and milk, and I'd like to eat

with you. I don't see any trouble about being glad about that."

"You don't seem to have any trouble being glad about everything," retorted Nancy, choking a little over her remembrance of Pollyanna's attempts to like the attic room.

"Well, that's the game, you know."

"The game?"

"Yes; the 'just being glad' game."

"Whatever are you talking about?"

"It's a game. Father told it to me," explained Pollyanna. "We've played it always, ever since I was a little girl."

"What is it?"

"We began it on some crutches that came in a missionary barrel."

"*Crutches!*"

"Yes. You see I'd wanted a doll, and Father had written to ask for one. But when the barrel came with the clothes and other things, the lady wrote that no dolls had been donated, but the little crutches had. So she sent them along as they might come in handy for some child, sometime. And that's when we began it."

"Well, I must say I can't see any game about that," declared Nancy, almost irritably.

"The game was to find something to be glad about," explained Pollyanna earnestly. "And we began right then on the crutches."

"Well, I can't see anything glad about getting a pair of crutches when you wanted a doll!"

"There is," Pollyanna cried. "I couldn't see either, Nancy, at first," she agreed with quick honesty. "Father had to tell it to me."

"Well then, suppose you tell me," Nancy almost snapped.

"Why, just be glad because you *don't* need 'em," declared Pollyanna, triumphantly. "You see it's easy when you know how!"

"Well, of all the queer doings!" breathed Nancy.

"Oh, but it isn't queer — it's lovely," maintained Pollyanna enthusiastically. "And we've played it ever since. The harder it is the more fun it is. Only sometimes it's almost too hard — like when your father dies and there isn't anybody but the Ladies' Aid left."

"Or when you're put in a snippy little room way at the top of the house with nothing in it," growled Nancy.

Pollyanna sighed.

"That was a hard one, at first," she admitted, "especially when I was so lonesome. I just didn't feel like playing the game, and I had been wanting pretty things so much! Then I happened to think how I hated to see my freckles in the looking glass, and I saw that lovely view out the window. Then I knew I'd found the things to be glad about."

"Humph!" Nancy tried to swallow the lump in her throat.

"Lots of times now I just play the game without thinking, you know. I've got so used to it. F-father and I used to like it so much," she faltered. "I suppose, though, it'll be a little harder now, I haven't anybody to play it with. Maybe Aunt Polly will play it, though," she added, as an afterthought.

"Her!" hissed Nancy behind her teeth. Then aloud she said doggedly: "See here, Miss Pollyanna, I ain't saying that I'll play it very well, and I ain't saying that I know how, anyway, but I'll play it with you after a fashion — I will!"

"Oh, Nancy!" Pollyanna gave her a rapturous hug. "That'll be splendid! Won't we have fun?"

"Er — maybe," conceded Nancy. "But you musn't count too much on me. I never was no case for games, but I'm a-going to make a most awful old try on this one. You're going to have someone to play it with, anyhow," she finished, as they entered the kitchen together.

Pollyanna ate her bread and milk with good appetite; then, at Nancy's suggestion, she went into the sitting room, where her aunt sat reading.

Miss Polly looked up coldly.

"Have you had your supper, Pollyanna?"

"Yes, Aunt Polly."

"I'm very sorry, Pollyanna, to have been obliged so soon to send you into the kitchen to eat bread and milk."

"I like bread and milk, and Nancy too. You mustn't feel one bit bad about that."

Aunt Polly suddenly sat a little more erect in her chair.

"Pollyanna, it's quite time you were in bed. You have had a hard day, and tomorrow we must plan your hours and go over your clothing to see what it is necessary to get for you. Nancy will give you a candle. Be careful how you handle it. Breakfast will be at half-past seven. See that you are down to that. Good night."

As a matter of course, Pollyanna went straight to her aunt's side and gave her an affectionate hug.

"I know I'm going to just love living with you — but then I knew I should before I came. Good night," Pollyanna called cheerfully, as she left the room.

"Well, upon my soul" exclaimed Miss Polly, half aloud. "What a most extraordinary child! She's glad I punished her, and I 'mustn't feel one bit bad,' and she's going to 'love to live' with me! Well, upon my soul!" exclaimed Miss Polly again, as she took up her book.

Fifteen minutes later, in the attic room, a lonely little girl sobbed into the tightly clutched sheet.

Downstairs in the kitchen, Nancy, hurrying with her work, jabbed the dish mop into the milk pitcher, and muttered:

"If playing a silly fool game about being glad you've got crutches when you want dolls is being a rock of refuge — why, I'm a-going to play it. I am, I am!"

A Question of Duty

Iᴛ ᴡᴀs ɴᴇᴀʀʟʏ seven o'clock when Pollyanna awoke that first day after her arrival. The little room was cooler now, as the air blew in fresh and sweet. Pollyanna saw that her aunt was already out among the rosebushes. With rapid fingers, she made herself ready to join her.

Down the attic stairs she sped, leaving both doors wide open. Through the hall, down the next flight, then bang through the front screened door she ran.

Aunt Polly was leaning over a rose bush when Pollyanna flung herself upon her.

"Oh, Aunt Polly, I'm glad this morning just to be alive!"

"Pollyanna!" remonstrated the lady, pulling herself as erect as she could with a weight of ninety pounds hanging about her neck. "Is this the usual way you say good morning?"

The little girl dropped to her toes.

"No, only when I love folks. I saw you from my window, Aunt Polly, and I got to thinking how you were my really truly aunt, and you looked so good I just had to come down and hug you!"

Thomas turned his back suddenly. Miss Polly attempted a frown.

"Pollyanna, you — I — Thomas, that will do for this morning. I think you understand — about those rosebushes," she said stiffly. Then she turned and walked rapidly away.

"Do you always work in the garden?" Pollyanna asked Thomas.

"Yes, Miss. I'm Old Tom, the gardner," he answered. He reached out a shaking hand and let it rest for a moment on her hair. "You are so like your mother. I used to know her when she was even littler than you. You see, I used to work in the garden then."

Pollyanna caught her breath audibly.

"You did? And you knew my mother, really. Oh, please tell me about her!" Pollyanna plumped down in the middle of the dirt path by the old man's side.

A bell sounded from the house and the next moment Nancy was seen flying out the back door.

"Miss Pollyanna, that bell means breakfast," she panted, pulling the little girl to her feet and hurrying her back to the house. "Other times it means other meals. But it always means that you're to run like time when you hear it, no matter where you are."

Breakfast for the first five minutes was a silent meal. Then Miss Polly, her disapproving eyes following the airy wings of two flies darting over the table, said sternly:

"Nancy, where did those flies come from?"

"I don't know, ma'am. There wasn't one in the kitchen."

"There are lots of them upstairs, Aunt Polly."

"What do you mean?" gasped Miss Polly. "Where did they come from?"

"Why, Aunt Polly, they came from outdoors, of course. Through the windows."

"You mean you raised those windows without any screens?"

"Why, yes. There weren't any screens there, Aunt Polly."

"Nancy," directed her mistress sharply, "you may set the muffins down and go at once to Miss Pollyanna's room and shut the windows. Shut the doors also. Later, when your morning work is done, go through every room with the spatter. See that you make a thorough search."

To her niece she said:

"Pollyanna, I have ordered screens for those windows. I knew, of course, that it was my duty to do that. But it seems to me that you have quite forgotten your duty."

"My duty?" Pollyanna's eyes were wide with wonder.

"Certainly. I know it is warm, but I consider it your duty to keep your windows closed till those screens come. Flies, Pollyanna, are not only unclean and annoying, but dangerous to health. After breakfast I will give you a little pamphlet on this matter to read."

"Oh, thank you, Aunt Polly. I love to read!"

Miss Polly drew in her breath audibly, then she shut her lips together hard. Pollyanna, seeing her stern face, offered an apology.

"I'm sorry, Aunt Polly," she said timidly. "I won't raise the windows again."

Her aunt made no reply. She did not speak again until the meal was over. Then she rose, went to the bookcase in the sitting room, took out a small paper booklet, and crossed the room to her niece's side.

"This is the article I spoke of, Pollyanna. I want you to go to your room at once and read it. I will be up in half an hour to look over your things."

Pollyanna, her eyes on the illustration of a fly's head, many times magnified, said delightedly, "Oh, thank you, Aunt Polly!" The next moment she skipped from the room, banging the door behind her.

Half an hour later, when Miss Polly entered Pollyanna's room, she was greeted with a burst of eager enthusiasm.

"Oh, Aunt Polly, I never saw anything so interesting in my life. I'm so glad you gave me this book to read! Why, I didn't know flies could carry such a lot of things on their feet, and — "

"That will do," observed Aunt Polly, with dignity. "Pollyanna, you may bring out your clothes now, and I will look them over. Those that are not suitable for you I shall give to the Sullivans, of course."

Pollyanna laid down the pamphlet and turned toward the closet.

"I'm afraid you'll think they're worse than the Ladies' Aid did — and they said they were shameful."

Pollyanna dived into her closet and brought out all the dresses. "They aren't nice, at all," she choked.

With the tips of her fingers Miss Polly

turned over the garments, so obviously made for somebody but Pollyanna. Next she bestowed her frowning attention on the patched undergarments in the bureau drawers.

"I've got the best ones on," confessed Pollyanna, anxiously.

Miss Polly did not seem to hear. Her scrutiny of the undergarments finished, she turned to Pollyanna somewhat abruptly.

"You have been to school, of course, Pollyanna?"

"Oh, yes, Aunt Polly. Besides Father — I mean, I was taught at home some too."

Miss Polly frowned.

"Very good. In the fall you will enter school of course. Mr. Hall, the principal, will no doubt settle in which grade you belong. Meanwhile, I suppose I ought to hear you read aloud half an hour each day."

"I love to read, but if you don't want to hear me I'd be just as glad to read to myself, Aunt Polly. I like best to read to myself — on account of the big words, you know."

"I don't doubt it," rejoined Miss Polly. "Have you studied music?"

"Not much. I learned to play the piano a little. Miss Gray — she plays for church — she taught me. But I'd just as soon let that go, Aunt Polly."

"Very likely," observed Aunt Polly, with slightly uplifted eyebrows. "Nevertheless, I think it is my duty to see that you are properly instructed in the rudiments of music. You sew, of course."

"Yes, ma'am." Pollyanna sighed. "The Ladies' Aid taught me that."

"You do *not* know how to cook, I presume."

"They were beginning to teach me that this summer, but I hadn't got far. I'd only learned chocolate fudge and fig cake, when I had to stop." Pollyanna's voice broke.

"Chocolate fudge and fig cake, indeed!" scorned Miss Polly. "I think we can remedy that very soon." She paused in thought for a minute, then went on slowly: "At nine o'clock every morning you will read aloud for one half hour to me. Before that you will use the time to put this room in order. Wednesday and Saturday forenoons, after half-past nine, you will spend with Nancy in the kitchen, learning to cook. Other mornings you will sew with me. That will leave the afternoons for your music. I shall, of course, procure a teacher at once for you," she said decisively, as she rose from her chair.

Pollyanna cried out in dismay.

"But, Aunt Polly, you haven't left me any time at all just to live."

"To live! What do you mean? As if you weren't living all the time."

"Oh, of course I'd be breathing, but I wouldn't be living. You breathe all the time you're asleep, but you aren't living. I mean living — doing the things you want to do: playing outdoors, reading, climbing hills, talking to Tom and Nancy, and finding out all about the houses and the people in the streets I came through yesterday. That's what I call living, Aunt Polly. Just breathing isn't living!"

Miss Polly lifted her head irritably.

"Pollyanna, you are the most extraordinary child! You will be allowed a proper amount of playtime, of course. But if I am willing to do my duty in seeing that you have proper care and instruction, you ought to be willing to do yours by seeing that that care and instruction are not ungratefully wasted."

Pollyanna looked shocked.

"Oh, Aunt Polly, as if I could ever be ungrateful to you. Why, I love you."

"Very well, then, see that you don't act ungrateful," vouchsafed Miss Polly, as she turned toward the door.

She had gone halfway down the stairs when a small, unsteady voice called after her:

"Please, Aunt Polly, you didn't tell me which

of my things you wanted to give away."

Aunt Polly emitted a sigh that ascended straight into Pollyanna's ears.

"Timothy will drive us into town at half-past one this afternoon. Not one of those garments is fit for my niece to wear. I should be very far from doing my duty by you if I let you appear in any one of them."

Now Pollyanna sighed. She believed she was going to hate that word duty.

In the hot little attic room she dropped onto one of the straight-backed chairs. For several minutes Pollyanna sat in silence, her eyes fixed on the forlorn heap of garments on the bed. Then slowly she rose and began to put away the dresses.

"There just isn't anything to be glad about that I can see," she said aloud, "unless — it's to be glad when the duty's done!" Whereupon she laughed suddenly.

Pollyanna and Punishments

FITTING POLLYANNA WITH a new wardrobe proved to be an exciting experience, more or less, for all concerned. Miss Polly came out of it with the feeling one might have at finding oneself on solid earth after a perilous walk across the thin crust of a volcano. The various clerks who had waited on Pollyanna and her aunt came out of it with enough amusing stories to keep their friends in gales of laughter the rest of the week. Pollyanna herself came out of it with radiant smiles and a heart content. As she expressed it to one of the clerks:

"When you haven't had anything but missionary barrels and Ladies' Aiders to give you clothes, it is perfectly lovely to walk right in and buy clothes that are brand-new and don't have to be tucked up or let down because they don't fit."

At half-past eight that night Pollyanna went up to bed. The screens had not yet come, and her room was like an oven. With longing eyes she looked at the two fast-closed windows, but she did not raise them. She undressed, folded her clothes neatly, said her prayers, blew out her candle, and climbed into bed.

Just how long she lay in sleepless misery she did not know, but it seemed to her that it must have been hours. Finally she slipped out of bed, felt her way across the room, and opened the door.

Out in the main attic was velvet blackness, save where the moon flung a path of silver halfway across the floor from the east dormer window. Ignoring the fearsome darkness to the right and to the left, Pollyanna drew a quick breath and walked straight into that silvery path, and over to the window.

She had hoped that this window might have a screen, but it did not. Outside, however, there was a wide world of fairylike beauty, and fresh, sweet air.

As she stepped nearer and peered longingly out, she saw something else: She saw the wide, flat tin roof of Miss Polly's sun parlor a little way below the window. The sight filled her with longing.

If only her bed were out there! Folks did sleep out of doors. Joel Hartley at home, who was so sick with consumption, had to sleep out of doors.

Suddenly Pollyanna remembered the row of long white bags hanging from nails near this attic window. Nancy had said that they contained winter clothing, put away for the summer. Pollyanna felt her way to these bags. She selected a nice fat soft one (it contained Miss Polly's sealskin coat) for a bed, a thinner one to be doubled up for a pillow, and still another (which was so thin it seemed almost empty) for a covering. Thus equipped, Pollyanna went back to the window, raised the sash, stuffed her burden through to the roof below, then let herself down after it, closing the window carefully behind her.

How deliciously cool it was! Pollyanna drew in long, full breaths of the refreshing air. The tin roof under her feet crackled with little resounding snaps. Pollyanna walked back and forth two or three times from end to end — it gave her such a pleasant sensation of airy space, and the roof was so broad and flat that she had no fear of falling off. Finally, with a sigh of contentment, she curled herself up on the sealskin-coat mattress, arranged one bag for a pillow and the other for a covering, and settled herself to sleep.

Downstairs, in her room next to the sun parlor, Miss Polly was hurrying into dressing gown and slippers, her face white and frightened. A minute before she had telephoned in a shaking voice to Timothy:

"Come up quick! — you and your father. Bring lanterns. Somebody is on the roof of the sun parlor. He must have climbed up the rose-trellis, and he can get right into the house through the east window in the attic. I have locked the attic door, but hurry, quick!"

Sometime later, Pollyanna, just dropping off to sleep, was startled by a flashing lantern and a trio of amazed voices. She opened her eyes to see Timothy at the top of a ladder, Old Tom just coming through the attic window, and her aunt peering out from behind him.

"Pollyanna, what does this mean?" cried Aunt Polly.

Pollyanna blinked and sat up.

"Why, Aunt Polly!" she stammered. "Don't look so scared! It's only that I was so hot in there. But I shut the window, Aunt Polly, so the flies couldn't get in."

Timothy disappeared down the ladder. Old Tom, with almost equal speed, handed his lantern to Miss Polly, and followed his son. Miss Polly bit her lip hard until the men were gone, then she said sternly:

"Pollyanna, hand those things to me at once and come in here. Of all the extraordinary children! For the rest of the night you are to sleep in my room with me. The screens will be here tomorrow, but until then I consider it my duty to keep you where I know where you are."

Pollyanna drew in her breath.

"In your room?" she cried rapturously. "Oh Aunt Polly, how lovely of you!"

There was no reply. To tell the truth, Miss Polly was feeling curiously helpless. For the third time since her niece's arrival, Miss Polly was punishing her — and for the third time she was being confronted with the amazing fact that her punishment was being taken as a special reward of merit. No wonder Miss Polly was feeling curiously helpless.

Pollyanna Pays a Visit

I᷇T WAS NOT LONG before life at the Harrington homestead settled into something like order. Pollyanna sewed, practiced her music, read aloud, and studied cooking in the kitchen. But she did not give any of these things as much time as had first been planned. Pollyanna had more time to "just live," as she expressed it. Almost every afternoon from two until six o'clock she did as she liked — provided she did not like to do things prohibited by Aunt Polly.

It is a question whether all this leisure time was given to Pollyanna as a relief from work — or as a relief for Aunt Polly. As those first July days passed, Miss Polly found occasion many times to exclaim, "What an extraordinary child!" and the reading and sewing lessons left her each day somewhat dazed and wholly exhausted.

Nancy, in the kitchen, fared better. She was not dazed or exhausted. Wednesdays and Saturdays came to be red-letter days to her.

There were no children in the immediate neighborhood of the Harrington homestead for Pollyanna to play with. The house itself was on the outskirts of the village, and though there were other houses not far away, they did not contain any boys or girls near Pollyanna's age. This, however, did not seem to disturb Pollyanna.

"Oh, no, I don't mind," she explained to Nancy. "I'm happy just to walk around and see the streets and the houses and watch the people. I just love people. Don't you Nancy?"

"Well I can't say I do — all of 'em," retorted Nancy.

Almost every pleasant afternoon found Pollyanna begging for "an errand to run," so that she might be off for a walk in one direction or another. It was on these walks that she frequently met the man. To herself Pollyanna always called him "the man," no matter if she met a dozen other men the same day.

The man often wore a long black coat and a high silk hat — two things that the other men never wore. His face was clean shaven and rather pale, and his hair, showing below his hat, was somewhat gray. He walked erect, and rather rapidly, and he was always alone. Perhaps it was because of this that Pollyanna one day spoke to him.

"How do you do, sir? Isn't it a nice day?" she said, as she approached him.

The man threw a hurried glance about him, then stopped uncertainly.

"Did you speak — to me?" he asked in a sharp voice.

"Yes, sir," replied Pollyanna. "I said it's a nice day, isn't it?"

"Eh? Oh! Humph!" he grunted, and strode on again.

Pollyanna laughed. He was such a funny man, she thought.

The next day she saw him again.

"It isn't quite so nice as yesterday, but it's pretty nice," she called out cheerfully.

"Eh? Oh! Humph!" grunted the man as before and once again Pollyanna laughed.

When Pollyanna accosted him in much the same manner for the third time, the man stopped abruptly.

"See here, child, who are you, and why are you speaking to me every day?"

"I'm Pollyanna Whittier, and I thought you

looked lonesome. I'm glad you stopped. Now we're introduced — only I don't know your name yet."

"Well, of all the — " The man did not finish his sentence, but strode on faster than ever.

"Maybe he didn't understand," Pollyanna murmured, as she proceeded on her way.

Pollyanna was carrying calf's-foot jelly to Mrs. Snow. Miss Polly Harrington always sent something to Mrs. Snow once a week. She said she thought it was her duty, inasmuch as Mrs. Snow was poor, sick, and a member of her church. Miss Polly usually did her duty by Mrs. Snow on Thursday afternoons — not personally, but through Nancy. Today Pollyanna had begged the privilege, and Nancy had promptly given it to her in accordance with Miss Polly's orders.

"And it's glad that I am to get rid of it," Nancy declared in private to Pollyanna; "though it's a shame to be tucking the job off on to you, poor lamb."

"But I'd love to do it, Nancy."

"You won't after you've done it once," predicted Nancy, sourly.

"Why not?"

"Because nobody does. If folks wasn't sorry for her there wouldn't be a soul would go near her from morning till night, she's that cantankerous. I pity her daughter what has to take care of her."

"But why, Nancy?"

"Well, in plain words, it's just that nothing that happens ever happens right in Miss Snow's eyes. If it's Monday she's bound to say she wishes it was Sunday. And if you take her jelly you're pretty sure to hear she wanted chicken. But if you did bring chicken, she'd be hankering for lamb broth!"

"Why, what a funny woman." Pollyanna laughed. "She must be so surprising and different. I love different folks."

"Humph! Well, Mrs. Snow's different all right — I hope, for the sake of the rest of us!" Nancy had finished grimly.

Pollyanna was thinking of these remarks as she turned in at the gate of the shabby little cottage.

A pale-faced, tired-looking young girl answered her knock at the door.

"How do you do?" began Pollyanna politely. "I'm from Miss Polly Harrington, and I'd like to see Mrs. Snow, please."

"Well, if you would, you're the first one that ever liked to see her," muttered the girl under her breath, but Pollyanna did not hear this. The girl had turned and was leading the way to a door at the end of the hall.

In the sickroom, after the girl had ushered her in and closed the door, Pollyanna blinked a little before she could accustom her eyes to the gloom. Then she saw a woman half sitting up in the bed across the room. Pollyanna advanced at once.

"How do you do, Mrs. Snow? Aunt Polly says she hopes you are comfortable today, and she's sent you some calf's-foot jelly."

"Dear me! Jelly?" murmured a fretful voice. "Of course I'm very much obliged, but I was hoping it would be lamb broth today."

"Why I thought it was chicken you wanted when folks brought you jelly," Pollyanna said.

"What?" The sick woman turned sharply.

"Nancy said it was chicken you wanted when we brought jelly, and lamb broth when we brought chicken."

The sick woman pulled herself up till she sat erect in the bed — a most unusual thing for her to do, though Pollyanna did not know this.

"Well, Miss Impertinence, who are you?" she demanded.

Pollyanna laughed.

"I'm Pollyanna Whittier, Miss Polly Harrington's niece, and I've come to live with her. That's why I'm here with the jelly today."

All through the first part of this sentence, the sick woman had sat erect, but at the reference to the jelly she fell back on her pillow listlessly.

"Very well, thank you. Your aunt is very kind, of course, but my appetite isn't very good this morning, and I was wanting lamb — " She stopped suddenly, then went on with an abrupt change of subject. "I never slept a wink last night — not a wink!"

"Oh dear, I wish I didn't," said Pollyanna, placing the jelly on the little stand and seating herself in the nearest chair. "You lose such a lot of time sleeping. Don't you think so?"

"Lose time sleeping!" exclaimed the sick woman.

"Yes, when you might be just living, you know. It seems such a pity we can't live nights too."

Once again the woman pulled herself erect in her bed.

"Well, if you ain't the amazing young one!" she cried. "Here! go to that window and pull up the shade," she directed. "I should like to know what you look like!"

Pollyanna rose to her feet.

"Oh, dear, then you'll see my freckles, won't you," she sighed, as she went to the window. "There! Now you can — oh!" she broke off, as she turned back to the bed. "They didn't tell me you were so pretty!"

"Me! — pretty!" scoffed the woman, bitterly.

"Why, yes. Didn't you know it?" cried Pollyanna.

"Well, no, I didn't," retorted Mrs. Snow dryly. Mrs. Snow had lived for forty years, and for fifteen of those years she had been too busy complaining to find much time to enjoy things as they were.

"Your eyes are big and dark, and your hair's dark too, and curly," said Pollyanna. Why, Mrs. Snow, you are pretty! I should think you'd know it when you looked at yourself in the glass."

"The glass!" snapped the sick woman, falling back on her pillow. "Yes, well, I ain't done much primping before the mirror these days — and you wouldn't, if you was flat on your back as I am."

"Why, no, of course not," agreed Pollyanna sympathetically. "But wait — just let me show you," she said going over to the bureau and picking up a small mirror.

On the way back to the bed she stopped, eyeing the sick woman with a critical gaze.

"If you don't mind, I'd like to fix your hair just a little before I let you see yourself," she

61

said. "May I fix your hair, please?"

"Why, I suppose so, if you want to," permitted Mrs. Snow grudgingly. "But it won't stay, you know."

"Oh, thank you. I love to fix people's hair," Pollyanna said, carefully laying down the mirror.

The sick woman, frowning prodigiously, and openly scoffing at the whole procedure, was beginning to tingle with a feeling perilously near to excitement.

"There!" declared Pollyanna finally. "Now I reckon you're ready to be looked at!" And she held out the mirror in triumph.

"I just love your hair fluffed out like that," Pollyanna said. "Don't you?"

"Hm-m; maybe. Still — 'twon't last, with me tossing back and forth on the pillow as I do."

"Of course not — and I'm glad too." Pollyanna nodded cheerfully. "Because then I can fix it again. Anyhow, I should think you'd be glad it's black — black shows up so much nicer than yellow hair like mine does."

"I never did set much store by black hair — shows gray too soon," retorted Mrs. Snow. She spoke fretfully, but she still held the mirror before her face.

"Oh, I love black hair. I should be so glad if I only had it," sighed Pollyanna.

Mrs. Snow dropped the mirror and turned irritably.

"Well, you wouldn't — not if you were me. You wouldn't be glad for black hair nor anything else — if you had to lie here all day as I do!"

"It would be kind of hard to do it then, wouldn't it?" Pollyanna mused aloud.

"Do what?"

"Be glad about things."

"Be glad about things — when you're sick in bed all your days? Well, I should say it would," retorted Mrs. Snow. "If you don't think so, just tell me something to be glad about, that's all!"

To Mrs. Snow's amazement, Pollyanna sprang to her feet and clapped her hands.

"Oh, good! That'll be a hard one. I've got to go now, but I'll think about it all the way home, and maybe the next time I come I can tell it to you. Good-by. I've had a lovely time! Good-by," she called again, as she went through the doorway.

"Well, I never!" sputtered Mrs. Snow, staring after her visitor. By and by she turned her head and picked up the mirror, eyeing her reflection critically.

"That little thing has got a knack with hair — and no mistake," she muttered under her breath. "I declare, I didn't know it could look so pretty. But then, what's the use?" she sighed, dropping the mirror into the bed-clothes, and rolling her head on the pillow fretfully.

A little later when Mrs. Snow's daughter came in, the mirror still lay among the bed-clothes, though it had been carefully hidden from sight.

"Why, Mother," Milly cried, "the shade is up!"

"Well, what if it is?" snapped the sick wom-an. "I needn't stay in the dark all my life even if I am sick, need I?"

"Why, n-no, of course not," Milly replied, as she reached for the medicine bottle. "It's only — well, I've tried to get you to have a lighter room for ages — and you wouldn't."

There was no reply to this. Mrs. Snow was picking at the lace on her nightgown. At last she spoke fretfully.

"I should think somebody might give me a new nightdress instead of lamb broth for a change!"

"Why, mother!"

No wonder Milly gasped aloud. In the drawer behind her lay two new nightdresses that Milly had been vainly urging her mother to wear for months.

Which Tells of the Man

It rained the next time Pollyanna saw the man.

"It isn't so nice today, is it?" she called.

The man did not even grunt this time, nor turn his head. Pollyanna decided that of course he did not hear her. The next time, therefore, which happened to be the following day, she spoke up louder.

"How do you do?" she called. "I'm glad it isn't yesterday, aren't you?"

The man stopped abruptly. There was an angry scowl on his face.

"See here, little girl, we might just as well settle this thing right now. I've got something besides the weather to think of. I don't know whether the sun shines or not."

"No, sir. I thought you didn't. That's why I told you."

"Eh? What?" he said sharply, in sudden understanding of her words.

"I said that's why I told you — so you would notice it. You know — that the sun shines, and all that. I knew you'd be glad it did if you only stopped to think of it."

"Well, of all the — " muttered the man, with an irritated gesture. He started to walk away but after the second step he turned back, still frowning.

"See here, why don't you find someone your own age to talk to?"

"I'd like to, but there aren't any around here, Nancy says. Still, I don't mind so very much. I like old folks just as well, maybe better sometimes — being used to the Ladies' Aid."

"Humph! The Ladies' Aid, indeed! Is that what you took me for?" The man's lips were threatening to smile.

"Oh, no, sir." Pollyanna laughed. "Not that you're not just as good of course — maybe better," she added in hurried politeness. "You see, I'm sure you're much nicer than you look!"

The man made a queer noise in his throat.

"Well, of all the — " he muttered again, as he turned and strode on as before.

The next time Pollyanna met the man, his eyes were gazing straight into hers with a quizzical directness that made his face look really pleasant.

"Good afternoon," he greeted her a little stiffly. "Perhaps I'd better say right away that I *know* the sun is shining today."

"But you don't have to tell me." Pollyanna nodded, brightly. "I knew you *knew* it just as soon as I saw you."

"Oh, you did, did you?"

"Yes, sir; I saw it in your eyes and in your smile."

"Humph!" grunted the man as he passed on.

After that the man always spoke to Pollyanna, and frequently he spoke first, though usually he only said good afternoon. Even that, however, was a great surprise to Nancy, who chanced to be with Pollyanna one day when the greeting was given.

"Sakes alive, Miss Pollyanna," she gasped. "Did that man *speak* to *you*?"

"Why, yes, he always does now," replied Pollyanna.

" 'He always does!' Goodness! Do you know who he is?" demanded Nancy.

Pollyanna shook her head.

"He forgot to tell me. I did my part of the introducing, but he didn't."

Nancy's eyes widened.

"But he never speaks to anybody — he hasn't for years, except when he just has to for business and all that. He's John Pendleton. He lives all by himself in the big house on Pendleton Hill. He won't even have anyone around to cook for him — comes down to the hotel for his meals three times a day. I know Sally Miner, who waits on him, and she says he hardly opens his mouth enough to tell her what he wants to eat. She has to guess it more'n half the time — only it'll be somethin' *cheap*! She knows that without no telling."

Pollyanna nodded sympathetically.

"I know. You have to look for cheap things when you're poor. Father and I took meals out a lot. We had beans and fish cakes mostly. We used to say how glad we were we liked beans. We said it especially when we were looking at the roast turkey plate. That was sixty cents. Does Mr. Pendleton like beans?"

"What if he does — or don't? Why, Miss Pollyanna, he ain't poor. He's got loads of money. There ain't nobody in town as rich as he is. He could eat dollar bills if he wanted to and not know it."

"As if *anybody* could eat dollar bills and not know it, Nancy."

"I mean he's rich enough to do it." Nancy shrugged. "He ain't spending his money, that's all. He's a-saving of it. But, say, it is queer, his speaking to you, Miss Pollyanna. He don't speak to no one, and he lives all alone in that great big house, all full of grand things, they say. Some says he's crazy, and some just cross; and some says he's got a skeleton in his closet."

"Oh, Nancy!" Pollyanna shuddered. "How could he keep such a dreadful thing? I should think he'd throw it away!"

Nancy chuckled. She knew that Pollyanna had taken the skeleton literally instead of figuratively, but she didn't correct the mistake.

"And *everybody* says he's mysterious," Nancy went on. "Some years he just travels, week in and week out, and it's always in countries like — Egypt and Asia and the Desert of Sarah, you know."

"Oh, a missionary." Pollyanna nodded.

"Well, I didn't say that, Miss Pollyanna. When he comes back he writes books — queer, odd books, they say, about some gimcrack he's found in them countries. But he don't never seem to want to spend no money here — leastways, not for just living."

"Of course not — if he's saving it for the missionaries," declared Pollyanna. "But he is a funny man, and he's different too, just like Mrs. Snow, only he's a different different."

"Well, I guess he is." Nancy chuckled.

"I'm more glad than ever, now, that he speaks to me," sighed Pollyanna contentedly.

A Surprise for Mrs. Snow

THE NEXT TIME Pollyanna went to see Mrs. Snow, she found that lady once again in a darkened room.

"It's the little girl from Miss Polly's, Mother," announced Milly, in a tired manner. Then Pollyanna found herself alone with the invalid.

"Oh, it's you, is it?" asked a fretful voice from the bed. "I remember you. Anybody'd remember you, I guess, if they saw you once. I wish you had come yesterday."

"Did you?" Pollyanna advanced into the room, and set her basket carefully down on a chair. "My but it's dark in here. I can't see you a bit," she said, crossing to the window and pulling up the shade. "I want to see if you've fixed your hair — oh, you haven't! Maybe you'll let me do it later, but now I want you to see what I've brought."

The woman stirred restlessly, but she turned her eyes toward the basket. "Well, what is it?"

"Guess! What do you want?" Pollyanna had moved back to the basket. Her face was alight.

"Why, I don't want anything, as I know of." The sick woman frowned. "After all, they all taste alike!"

"This won't. Guess! If you did want something, what would it be?"

The woman hesitated. She was so accustomed to wanting what she did not have that to state what she *did* want seemed impossible — until she knew what she had. Obviously, however, she must say something.

"Well, there's lamb broth — "

"I've got it!" crowed Pollyanna.

"But that's what I didn't want," Mrs. Snow complained, sure now of what her stomach craved. "It was chicken I wanted."

"I've got that too," cried Pollyanna.

The woman turned in amazement.

"Both of them?" she demanded.

"Yes — and calf's-foot jelly," Pollyanna declared triumphantly. "Of course there's only a little of each — but there's some of all of 'em!"

There was no reply. The sick woman seemed to be trying — mentally — to find something she had lost.

"There!" announced Pollyanna, as she arranged the three bowls in a row on the table. "Like enough it'll be lamb broth you'll want tomorrow. How are you today?" she finished in polite inquiry.

"Very poorly, thank you," murmured Mrs. Snow, falling back into her usual listless attitude. "I lost my nap this morning. Nellie Higgins next door has begun music lessons, and her practicing drives me nearly wild. She was at it all the morning — every minute! I'm sure, I don't know what I shall do!"

"I know." Pollyanna nodded sympathetically. "It is awful! Mrs. White had it once — one of my Ladies' Aiders, you know. She had rheumatic fever too, so she couldn't thrash around. She said it would have been easier if she could have. Can you?"

"Can I what?"

"Thrash around — move, you know, when the music gets too hard to stand."

Mrs. Snow stared a little.

"Why of course I can move anywhere — in bed," she added a little irritably.

"Well, you can be glad of that then, can't

you?" queried Pollyanna. "But Mrs. White couldn't. She told me afterward she reckoned she'd have gone crazy if it hadn't been for Mr. White's sister's ears."

"Sister's ears! What do you mean?"

"You see, Miss White was deaf — awfully deaf, and she came to help take care of Mrs. White and the house. Well, they had such an awful time making her understand anything, that every time the piano commenced to play across the street, Mrs. White was glad she could hear it. She didn't mind so much, you see, 'cause she couldn't help thinking how awful it would be if she was deaf like her husband's sister, and couldn't hear anything. You see, she was playing the game. I'd told her about it."

"The game?"

Pollyanna clapped her hands.

"I forgot. Mrs. Snow, I've thought up what you can be glad about."

"*Glad* about! What do you mean?"

"Don't you remember? You asked me to tell you something you could be glad about, even though you had to lie here in bed all day."

"Oh, that," scoffed the woman. "Yes, I remember, but I didn't suppose you were in earnest any more than I was."

"Oh, yes, I was," replied Pollyanna, "and I found it too. I will own up that I couldn't think of anything for a while. Then I got it."

"Did you, really? Well, what is it?" Mrs. Snow's voice was sarcastically polite.

Pollyanna drew a long breath.

"I thought how glad you could be that other folks weren't like you — sick in bed like this," she announced impressively.

Mrs. Snow stared. Her eyes were angry.

"Well, really!" she exclaimed, in a not very agreeable tone of voice.

"And now I'll tell you the game," continued Pollyanna, blithely confident. "It'll be hard, but there's so much more fun when it is hard! You see, it's like this." She told about the missionary barrel, the crutches, and the doll that did not come.

The story was just finished when Milly appeared at the door.

"Your aunt is wanting you, Miss Pollyanna," she said with dreary listlessness. "She telephoned down to the Harlows' across the way. She says you're to hurry — that you've got some practicing to make up before dark."

Pollyanna reluctantly rose.

"I suppose I ought to be glad I've got legs to hurry with, hadn't I Mrs. Snow?"

There was no answer. Mrs. Snow's eyes were closed. But Milly, whose eyes were wide open, saw that there were tears on her mother's cheeks.

"Good-by," Pollyanna called over her shoulder, as she reached the door. "I'm sorry about the hair — I wanted to do it. But maybe I can next time!"

One by one the July days passed. To Pollyanna they were happy days. She often told her aunt how very happy they were. Whereupon her aunt would usually reply wearily:

"Very well, Pollyanna. I am gratified, of course, but I trust that they are profitable as well — otherwise I should have failed in my duty."

Generally Pollyanna would answer this with a hug and a kiss — a proceeding that was still most disconcerting to Miss Polly. But one day she questioned her aunt. It was during the sewing hour.

"Do you mean that it wouldn't be enough, that they should be just happy days?" she asked wistfully.

"That is what I mean, Pollyanna."

"They must be profitable as well?"

"Certainly."

"What is being profitable?"

"Why, it — it's just being profitable — having profit, something to show for it, Pollyanna."

"Then just being glad isn't profitable?" Pollyanna asked, a little anxiously.

"Certainly not."

"Oh dear! Then you wouldn't like it. I'm afraid you won't ever play the game, Aunt Polly."

"Game? What game?"

"Why, that Father — " Pollyanna pressed her hands to her lips. "N-nothing," she stammered.

Miss Polly frowned.

"That will do for this morning, Pollyanna," she said tersely. And the sewing lesson was over.

It was that afternoon that Pollyanna, coming down from her attic room, met her aunt on the stairway.

"Why, Aunt Polly, how lovely!" she cried. "You were coming up to see me! I love company," she finished, running up the stairs and throwing her door wide open.

Now Miss Polly had not been intending to visit her niece. She had been planning to look for a certain white wool shawl in the cedar chest near the east window. But to her unbounded surprise, she found herself in Pollyanna's room sitting in one of the straight-backed chairs. Miss Polly had found herself like this, doing some utterly unexpected, surprising thing, so many times since Pollyanna had come.

"I love company," said Pollyanna again. "Especially since I've had this room, all mine, you know. I do own this room, don't I?"

"Why, y-yes, Pollyanna," murmured Miss Polly, vaguely wondering why she did not get up and go look for that shawl.

"I just love this room, even if it hasn't got the carpets and curtains and pictures I'd been want—" With a painful blush Pollyanna stopped short.

"What's that, Pollyanna?"

"N-nothing, Aunt Polly. I didn't mean to say it."

"Probably not," returned Miss Polly, coldly, "but you did say it, so suppose we have the rest of it."

"But it wasn't anything, only that I'd been kind of planning on pretty carpets and lace curtains and things, you know. But, of course—"

"*Planning* on them!" interrupted Miss Polly, sharply.

Pollyanna blushed still more painfully.

"I ought not to have, Aunt Polly," she apologized. "It was only because I'd always wanted them and hadn't had them, I suppose. Oh, we had rugs, but they were little, you know, and one had ink spots, and the other holes. And there were only those two pictures. The one

Father — I mean the good one we sold, and the bad one that broke. Of course if it hadn't been for all that, I shouldn't have wanted them so — pretty things, I mean. I shouldn't have got to planning that first day how pretty mine would be here and — and — "

Miss Polly rose suddenly to her feet. Her face was very red.

"That will do, Pollyanna," she said stiffly. "You have said quite enough." The next minute she was going down the stairs — and not until she reached the first floor did it suddenly occur to her that she had gone up into the attic to find a white wool shawl.

Less than twenty-four hours later, Miss Polly said to Nancy:

"Nancy, you may move Miss Pollyanna's things downstairs this morning to the room directly beneath. I have decided to have my niece sleep there for the present."

"Yes, ma'am," Nancy said aloud. "Oh, glory!" said Nancy to herself.

To Pollyanna, a minute later, she cried joyously: "You're to sleep downstairs in the room straight under this. You are — you are!"

Pollyanna actually grew white.

"You mean — why, Nancy, not really — really and truly?"

Nancy nodded her head to Pollyanna over the armful of dresses she had taken from the closet. "I'm told to take down your things, and I'm going to take 'em too, before she gets a chance to change her mind."

Pollyanna did not stop to hear the end of this sentence. She was flying downstairs, two steps at a time. Bang went two doors and a chair before Pollyanna at last reached her goal — Aunt Polly.

"Oh, Aunt Polly, Aunt Polly, did you mean it, really? Why, that's the room's got *everything* — the carpet and curtains and three pictures. Oh, Aunt Polly!"

"Very well, Pollyanna. I am gratified that you like the change, of course, and if you think so much of all those things, I trust you will take proper care of them. Now, please pick up that chair. And you have banged two doors in the last half-minute." Miss Polly spoke sternly because, for some inexplicable reason, she felt inclined to cry — and Miss Polly was not used to feeling inclined to cry.

Pollyanna picked up the chair.

"Aunt Polly, did you ever bang doors?"

"I hope not, Pollyanna."

"Why, Aunt Polly, what a shame!" Pollyanna's face expressed only concerned sympathy.

"A shame!" repeated Aunt Polly, too dazed to say more.

"Why, yes. If you didn't, that must have

79

meant that you weren't ever glad over anything — or you would have banged 'em. You
couldn't have helped it. And I'm so sorry you
weren't ever glad over anything!"

"Pollyanna!" But Pollyanna was gone, and
only the distant bang of the attic door answered her.

Miss Polly, in the sitting room, felt vaguely
disturbed. Of course she had been glad — over
some things!

Introducing Jimmy

A UGUST CAME. August brought several surprises and some changes — none of which were really a surprise to Nancy. Since Pollyanna's arrival, Nancy had come to look for surprises and changes.

First there was the kitten.

Pollyanna found the kitten mewing pitifully some distance down the road. When systematic questioning of the neighbors failed to find anyone who claimed it, Pollyanna brought it home at once.

"I was glad I didn't find anyone who owned it," she told her aunt, "because I wanted to bring it home all the time. I love kittens. I knew you'd be glad to let it live here."

Miss Polly looked at the forlorn gray bunch of misery in Pollyanna's arms, and shivered. Miss Polly did not care for cats — not even pretty, healthy, clean ones.

"Ugh! Pollyanna! What a dirty little beast! And it's sick, I'm sure, and all mangy and flea-y."

"I know it, poor little thing," crooned Pollyanna, looking into the little creature's frightened eyes. "And it's all trembly too, it's so scared. It doesn't know that we're going to keep it."

"No — nor does anybody else," retorted Miss Polly, with meaning emphasis.

"Oh, yes, they do," replied Pollyanna, misunderstanding her aunt's words. "I told everybody we should keep it, if I didn't find where it belonged. I knew you'd be glad to have it — poor little lonesome thing!"

Miss Polly opened her lips and tried to speak. But the curious helpless feeling had her once again in its grip.

"Of course I knew," Pollyanna hurried on gratefully, "that you wouldn't let a little kitten go hunting for a home, and I said so to Mrs. Ford when she asked if you'd let me keep it. I knew you'd feel that way," she finished happily, as she ran from the room.

"But Pollyanna," called Miss Polly. "I don't — " But Pollyanna was already halfway to the kitchen calling: "Nancy, Nancy, just see this dear little kitten."

Aunt Polly, who abhorred cats, fell back in her chair with a gasp of dismay, powerless to object.

The next day it was a dog, even dirtier and more forlorn than the kitten, but again Miss Polly, to her dumbfounded amazement, found herself figuring as a kind of angel of mercy.

When Pollyanna brought home a small, ragged boy, and confidently claimed the same protection for him, Miss Polly, however, did have something to say. It happened this way:

On a pleasant Thursday morning Pollyanna had been returning from Mrs. Snow's house. Mrs. Snow and Pollyanna were the best of friends now. Their friendship had started from the third visit Pollyamna had made, the one after she told Mrs. Snow the game.

Pollyanna was thinking of this now when suddenly she saw the boy. He was sitting by the roadside, whittling half-heartedly at a small stick.

"Hullo," said Pollyanna.

The boy glanced up, but looked away again at once.

"Hullo, yourself," he mumbled.

"You don't look as if you'd be glad even for calf's-foot jelly," Pollyanna said, stopping before him.

The boy stirred restlessly, gave her a surprised look, and began to whittle again at his stick, with the dull, broken-bladed knife in his hand.

Pollyanna hesitated, then dropped down on the grass near him.

"My name's Pollyanna Whittier," she began pleasantly. "What's yours?"

Again the boy stirred restlessly. He almost got to his feet, but he settled back.

"Jimmy Bean," he grunted.

"Good! Now we're introduced. I live at Miss Polly Harrington's house. Where do you live?"

"Nowhere."

"Nowhere! Why, you can't — everybody lives somewhere," asserted Pollyanna.

"Well, I don't — just now. I'm hunting up a new place."

"Oh! Where is it?"

The boy regarded her with scornful eyes.

"Silly! As if I'd be hunting for it if I knew!"

Pollyanna tossed her head a little. She did not like to be called "silly." Still, this boy was somebody to talk to besides old folks.

"Where did you live before?" she queried.

"If you ain't the one for asking questions," the boy said impatiently.

"I have to be," retorted Pollyanna calmly, "or else I couldn't find out a thing about you. If you'd talk more, I wouldn't talk so much."

The boy gave a short laugh. It was not quite a willing one, but his face looked a little pleasanter when he spoke this time.

"All right then — here goes! I'm Jimmy Bean, and I'm ten years old going on eleven. I come last year to live at the orphans' home, but they've got so many kids there ain't much room for me. So I've quit. I'm going to live somewheres else — but I ain't found the place, yet. I'd like a home, with a mother in it, you know, instead of a matron. If you has a home, you has folks, and I ain't had folks since Dad died. I've tried four houses but they didn't want me, though I said I expected to work. Is that all you want to know?" The boy's voice had broken a little over the last two sentences.

"What a shame!" sympathized Pollyanna. "I know how you feel, because after my father died there wasn't anybody but the Ladies' Aid for me, until Aunt Polly said she'd take — " Pollyanna stopped abruptly. The dawning of a wonderful idea began to show in her face.

"Oh, I know just the place for you," she cried. "Aunt Polly'll take you. I know she will! Didn't she take me? And didn't she take Fluffy and Buffy, when they didn't have anyone to love them, or any place to go? — and they're only

85

cats and dogs. Oh, come, I know Aunt Polly'll take you! You don't know how good and kind she is!"

Jimmy Bean's thin face brightened.

"Honest? Would she, now? I'd work, you know, an' I'm real strong!"

"Of course she would! Why, my Aunt Polly is the nicest lady in the world And there's rooms — heaps of 'em," Pollyanna continued, springing to her feet, and tugging at his arm. "It's an awful big house. Maybe, though," she added as they hurried on, "maybe you'll have to sleep in the attic room. I did, at first."

When the house was reached, Pollyanna piloted her companion straight into the presence of her aunt.

"Oh, Aunt Polly," she exclaimed. "Just look here! I've got something ever so much nicer than a kitten or a dog for you to bring up. It's a real live boy. He won't mind a bit sleeping in the attic."

Miss Polly grew white, then very red. She did not entirely understand, but she thought she understood enough.

"Pollyanna, what does this mean?" she demanded sharply.

Jimmy fell back a step and looked toward the door.

"Well, what is he doing here?"

"Why, Aunt Polly, I just told you!" Polly-anna's eyes were wide with surprise. "He's for you. I brought him home — so he could live here. He wants a home and folks. I told him how good you were to me and that I knew you would be to him."

Miss Polly dropped back in her chair and raised a shaking hand to her throat. The old helplessness was threatening once more to overcome her. With a visible struggle, however, she pulled herself erect.

"That will do, Pollyanna. This is the most absurd thing you've done yet. As if tramp cats and mangy dogs weren't bad enough, you bring home ragged little beggars from the street, who — "

There was a sudden stir from the boy. His eyes flashed and his chin came up. He confronted Miss Polly fearlessly.

"I ain't a beggar, marm, and I don't want nothing of you. I was calculating to work for my board an' keep. I wouldn't have come to your old house, anyhow, if this here girl hadn't made me, telling me how you was so good and kind that you'd be just dying to take me in. So, there!" He wheeled about and stalked from the room.

"Oh, Aunt Polly," choked Pollyanna. "I

thought you'd be glad to have him here! I should think you'd be glad — "

Miss Polly raised her hand in a preemptory gesture of silence. Her nerves had snapped at last. The "good and kind" of the boy's words were still ringing in her ears.

"Pollyanna," she cried sharply "will you stop using that everlasting word glad! It's glad — glad — glad from morning till night until I think I shall grow wild!"

From sheer amazement Pollyanna's jaw dropped.

"Why, Aunt Polly," she breathed, "I should think you'd be glad to have me gl — Oh!" she broke off, and hurried blindly from the room.

Before the boy had reached the end of the driveway, Pollyanna overtook him.

"I want you to know how sorry I am," she panted, catching him with a detaining hand.

"Sorry nothing. I ain't blaming you," retorted the boy, sullenly. "But I ain't no beggar!" he added, with sudden spirit.

"Of course you aren't! But you mustn't blame Auntie," appealed Pollyanna. "Probably I didn't do the introducing right. And I didn't tell her much about who you were. She *is* good and kind, really — she's always been. I do wish I could find some place for you though!"

The boy shrugged his shoulders and half turned away.

"Never mind. I guess I can find one myself. I ain't no beggar, you know."

Pollyanna was frowning thoughtfully.

"Say, I'll tell you what I'll do! The Ladies' Aid meets this afternoon. I heard Aunt Polly say so. I'll lay your case before them. That's what Father always did, when he wanted anything like new carpets, you know."

The boy turned fiercely.

"Well I ain't a new carpet. Besides — what is a Ladies' Aid?"

Pollyanna stared in shocked disapproval.

"Why, Jimmy Bean, wherever have you been brought up? — not to know what a Ladies' Aid is!"

"Oh, all right — if you ain't telling," grunted the boy, turning and beginning to walk away indifferently.

Pollyanna sprang to his side at once.

"It's — it's — why, it's just a lot of ladies that meet and sew and give suppers and raise money and talk — that's what a Ladies' Aid is. They're awfully kind — that is most of mine was back home. I haven't seen this one here, but they're always good, I reckon. I'm going to tell them about you this afternoon."

Again the boy spoke fiercely.

"Not much you will! Maybe you think I'm going to stand around an' hear a whole lot of women call me a beggar. Not much!"

"Oh, but you wouldn't be there," argued Pollyanna, quickly. "I'd go alone and tell them."

"You would?"

"Yes, and I'd tell it better this time," Pollyanna assured him, quick to see the signs of relenting in the boy's face. "And there'd be some of 'em, I know, that would be glad to give you a home."

"I'd work — don't forget to say that," cautioned the boy.

"Of course not," promised Pollyanna, sure now that her point was gained. "Then I'll let you know tomorrow."

"Where?"

"By the road — where I found you today, near Mrs. Snow's house."

"All right. I'll be there." The boy paused before he went on slowly: "Maybe I'd better go back to the Home for tonight. You see I ain't got no other place to stay, and I didn't leave till this morning. I slipped out. I didn't tell 'em I wasn't coming back, else they'd pretend I couldn't come — though I'm thinking they won't do no worrying when I don't show up sometime. They ain't like folks, you know. They don't care!"

"I know," nodded Pollyanna, with understanding. "But I'm sure, when I see you tomorrow, I'll have a home and folks that do care all ready for you. Good-by!" she called brightly, as she turned toward the house.

In the sitting room window at that moment, Miss Polly, who had been observing the two children, watched the boy until a bend of the road hid him from sight. Then she sighed, turned, and walked listlessly upstairs. Miss Polly did not usually move listlessly. In her ears rang the boy's scornful "you was so good and kind." In her heart was a curious sense of desolation — as of something lost.

Before the Ladies' Aid

Dinner, which came at noon in the Harrington homestead, was a silent meal on the day of the Ladies' Aid meeting. Pollyanna tried to talk, but she did not make a success of it, because four times she was obliged to break off her conversation in the middle of a "glad," much to her blushing discomfort. The fifth time it happened, Miss Polly moved her head wearily.

"There, there, child, say it, if you want to." I'm sure I'd rather you did than not if it's going to make all this fuss."

Pollyanna's face cleared.

"Oh, thank you. I'm afraid it would be

pretty hard not to say it. You see I've played it so long."

"You've what?" asked Aunt Polly.

"Played it — the game, you know, that Father — " Pollyanna stopped with a painful blush at finding herself so soon again on forbidden ground.

Aunt Polly frowned and said nothing. The rest of the meal was a silent one.

Pollyanna was not sorry to hear Aunt Polly tell the minister's wife over the telephone, a little later, that she would not be at the Ladies' Aid meeting owing to a headache.

Pollyanna knew that the Ladies' Aid met at two o'clock in the chapel next to the church, not quite half a mile from home. She planned to get there a little before three.

"I want them all to be there," she said to herself. "Else the very one that wasn't there might be the one who would be wanting to give Jimmy Bean a home."

Quietly, but with confident courage, Pollyanna ascended the chapel steps, pushed open the door, and entered the vestibule. A soft babel of chatter and laughter came from the main room. Hesitating only a brief moment Pollyanna pushed open one of the inner doors.

The chatter dropped to a surprised hush.

Pollyanna advanced a little timidly. Now that the time had come, she felt unwontedly shy.

"How do you do, Ladies' Aiders?" she faltered politely. "I'm Pollyanna Whittier. I reckon some of you know me, maybe. Anyway, I know you — only I don't know you all together this way."

The silence could almost be felt now. Some of the ladies did know this rather extraordinary niece of their fellow member, and nearly all had heard of her, but none of them could think of anything to say just then.

"I — I've come to — to lay the case before you," stammered Pollyanna, unconsciously falling into her father's familiar phraseology.

There was a slight rustle.

"Did your aunt send you, my dear?" asked Mrs. Ford, the minister's wife.

"Oh, no. I came all by myself," Pollyanna answered. "You see, I'm used to Ladies' Aiders. It was Ladies' Aiders that brought me up — with Father."

Somebody tittered, and the minister's wife frowned.

"Yes, dear. What is it?"

"Well, it — it's Jimmy Bean," began Pollyanna. "He hasn't any home except the orphan one, and they're full and don't want him anyhow, he thinks, so he wants another. He wants one of the common kind, that has a mother instead of a matron — folks, you know, that'll care. He's ten years old going on eleven. I thought some of you might like him — to live with you, you know."

"Well, did you ever!" murmured a voice, breaking the dazed pause that followed Pollyanna's words.

With anxious eyes Pollyanna swept the circle of faces about her.

"Oh, I forgot to say he will work," she added.

Still there was silence. Then coldly, one or two women began to question her. After a time they all had the story and began to talk among themselves, animatedly, not quite pleasantly.

Pollyanna listened with growing anxiety. Some of what was said she could not understand. She did gather after a time, however, that there was no woman there who had a home to give him, though every woman seemed to think that one of the others might take him, as there were several who had no little boys of their own already in their homes. But there was no one who agreed herself to take him. Then Pollyanna heard the minister's wife suggest timidly that the society might perhaps assume his support and education, instead of sending quite so much money this year to the little boys far away in India.

A great many ladies talked then, and several of them talked at once, even more loudly and more unpleasantly than before. It seemed that their society was famous for its offering to Hindu missions, and several said they should die of mortification if it should be less this year. Some of what was said Pollyanna thought she could not have understood correctly, for it sounded as if they did not care what the money did so long as the name of their society headed the list in a certain report. It was all very confusing, and not quite pleasant, so that Pollyanna was glad when she found herself outside again.

She was very sorry too, for it was not going to be easy to tell Jimmy Bean that the Ladies' Aid had decided that they would rather send all their money to bring up little India boys than save out enough to bring up one little boy in their own town. For which they could not get "a bit of credit in the report," according to the lady who wore spectacles.

"I should want them to send some money there," said Pollyanna to herself, as she trudged sorrowfully along. "But they acted as if little boys here weren't any account — only little boys way off. I should think they'd rather see Jimmy Bean grow — than just a report!"

In Pendleton Woods

POLLYANNA HAD NOT TURNED her steps toward home when she left the chapel. She had turned them instead toward Pendleton Hill.

"I don't have to get home till half-past five, anyway," she was telling herself; "and it'll be much nicer to go around by the way of the woods, even if I do have to climb to get there."

It was very beautiful in the Pendleton Woods, as Pollyanna knew by experience. But today, it seemed even more delightful, notwithstanding her disappointment over what she must tell Jimmy Bean tomorrow.

"I wish they were up here — all those ladies who talked so loud," Pollyanna said to herself, raising her eyes to the patches of vivid blue between the sunlit green of the treetops. "Anyhow, if they were up here, I reckon they'd change and take Jimmy Bean for their little boy." She was secure in this conviction, but unable to give a reason for it, even to herself.

Suddenly Pollyanna lifted her head and listened. A dog had barked some distance ahead. A moment later he came dashing toward her, still barking.

"Hullo, doggie — hullo!" Pollyanna snapped her fingers at the dog and looked expectantly down the path. She had seen the dog before, she was sure. He had been with the man, Mr. John Pendleton. She was looking now, hoping to see him. For some minutes she watched eagerly, but the man did not appear. Then she turned her attention toward the dog.

The dog, as even Pollyanna could see, was acting strangely. He was giving little short, sharp yelps, and running back and forth in the path ahead of her. Soon they reached a side path, and the little dog fairly flew down this, only to come back at once, whining and barking.

"That isn't the way home," Pollyanna said, keeping to the main path.

The little dog seemed frantic now. Back and forth, back and forth, between Pollyanna and the side path he vibrated, barking and whining pitifully. Every quiver of his little brown body, and every glance from his beseeching brown eyes were eloquent with appeal — so eloquent that at last Pollyanna turned, and followed him.

Straight ahead now, the little dog dashed madly, and it was not long before Pollyanna came upon the reason for it all. A man was lying motionless at the foot of a steep, overhanging mass of rock a few yards from the side path.

A twig cracked sharply under Pollyanna's foot, and the man turned his head. With a cry of dismay Pollyanna ran to his side.

"Mr. Pendleton! Are you hurt?"

"Hurt? Oh, no! I'm just taking a siesta in the sunshine," snapped the man irritably. "See here, how much do you know? What can you do? Have you got any sense?"

Pollyanna caught her breath with a little gasp, but — as was her habit — she answered the questions literally, one by one.

"Why, Mr. Pendleton, I don't know so very much, and I can't do a great many things, but most of the Ladies' Aiders, except Mrs. Rawson, said I had real good sense."

The man smiled grimly.

"There, there, child, I beg your pardon. It's only this confounded leg of mine. Now listen." He paused, and with some difficulty reached his hand into his trousers pocket and brought out a bunch of keys, singling out one between his thumb and forefinger. "Straight through the path there, about five minutes' walk, is my house. This key will admit you to the side door under the porte cochere. Do you know what a porte cochere is?"

"Oh, yes, sir. Auntie has one with a sun parlor over it. That's the roof I slept on — only I didn't. They found me."

"Eh? Oh! Well, when you get into the house, go straight through the vestibule and hall to the door at the end. On the big, flat-topped desk in the middle of the room you'll find a telephone. Do you know how to use a telephone"

"Oh, yes, sir! Why, once when Aunt Polly — "

"Never mind Aunt Polly now," cut in the man. "Hunt up Dr. Thomas Chilton's number on the card you'll find somewhere around there — it ought to be on the hook down at the side, but it probably won't be. You know a telephone card, I suppose, when you see one!"

"Oh, yes, sir!"

"Tell Dr. Chilton that John Pendleton is at the foot of Little Eagle Ledge in Pendleton Woods with a broken leg, and to come at once with a stretcher and two men. He'll know what to do besides that. Tell him to come by the path from the house."

"A broken leg? Oh, Mr. Pendleton, how perfectly awful!" cried Pollyanna. "But I'm so glad I came! Can't *I* do — "

"Yes, you can — but evidently you won't! Will you go and do what I ask and stop talking," moaned the man. With a little sobbing cry, Pollyanna went.

It was not long before she came in sight of the house. She had seen it before, though never so near as this. She was almost frightened now at the massiveness of the great pile of gray stone with its pillared verandas and its imposing entrance. Pausing only a moment, however, she sped across the big neglected lawn and around the house to the side door under the porte cochere. Her fingers were stiff from clutching the keys, but at last the bolt in the lock turned and the heavy, carved door swung slowly back on its hinges.

Pollyanna caught her breath. In spite of her feeling of haste, she paused a moment and looked fearfully through the vestibule to the wide, somber hall beyond. This was John Pendleton's house — the house of mystery, the house into which no one but its master entered, the house which sheltered, somewhere, a skeleton.

Pollyanna, looking neither to the right nor the left, fairly ran through the hall to the door at the end and opened it.

The room was large and somber like the hall. But through the west window, the sun threw a long shaft of gold across the floor that gleamed dully on the tarnished brass andirons in the fireplace and touched the nickel of the telephone on the great desk in the middle of the room. It was toward this desk that Pollyanna hurriedly tiptoed.

The telephone card was not on its hook, it was on the floor. But Pollyanna found it, and ran her shaking forefinger down through the C's to "Chilton." In due time she had Dr. Chilton at the other end of the wire, and was delivering her message and answering the doctor's terse, pertinent questions. This done, she hung up the receiver and drew a long breath of relief.

Pollyanna gave only a brief glance about her. With a confused vision in her eyes of crimson draperies, book-lined walls, a littered floor, an untidy desk, innumerable closed doors, and everywhere dust, dust, dust, she fled back through the hall to the great carved door, still half open as she had left it.

In what seemed an incredibly short time, Pollyanna was back in the woods at the man's side.

"Well, what is the trouble? Couldn't you get in?" he demanded.

"Why, of course I could!" Pollyanna answered. "As if I'd be here if I hadn't got in! And the doctor will be right up just as soon as possible with the men and things. He said he knew just where you were, so I didn't stay to show him. I wanted to be with you."

"Did you?" smiled the man grimly. "Well, I can't say I admire your taste."

"Do you mean — because you're so cross?"

"Thanks for your frankness. Yes."

Pollyanna laughed softly.

"But you're only cross outside. You aren't cross inside a bit!"

"Indeed! How do you know that?" asked the man, trying to change the position of his head without moving the rest of his body.

"Oh, lots of ways. There's — like that — the way you act with the dog," she said, pointing to the long, slender hand that rested on the dog's sleek head. "It's funny how dogs and cats know the insides of folks better than other folks do, isn't it? Say, I'm going to hold your head," she said abruptly.

The man winced several times and groaned once softly while the change was being made. But in the end he found Pollyanna's lap a very welcome substitute for the rocky hollow in which his head had lain before.

"That is better," he murmured faintly.

He did not speak again for some time. Pollyanna, watching his face, wondered if he was asleep. She did not think he was. He looked as if his lips were tight shut to keep back moans of pain.

Minute by minute the time passed. The sun dropped lower in the west and the shadows grew deeper under the trees. Pollyanna sat so still she hardly seemed to breathe. A bird alighted fearlessly within reach of her hand, and a squirrel whisked his bushy tail on a tree branch almost under her nose — yet with his bright little eyes all the while on the motionless dog.

At last the dog pricked up his ears and whined softly. Then he gave a short, sharp bark. The next moment Pollyanna heard voices, and very soon their owners appeared — three men carrying a stretcher and various other articles.

The tallest of the party, a smooth-shaven, kind-eyed man whom Pollyanna knew by sight as Dr. Chilton, advanced cheerily.

"Well, my little lady, playing nurse?"

"Oh, no, sir," Pollyanna assured him. "I've only held his head. I haven't given him a mite of medicine. But I'm glad I was here."

"So am I," said the doctor, as he turned his absorbed attention to the injured man.

Just a Matter of Jelly

POLLYANNA WAS LATE for supper on the night of the accident to John Pendleton but, as it happened, she escaped without reproof.

Nancy met her at the door.

"Well, if I ain't glad to be setting my two eyes on you. It's half past six!"

"I know it," admitted Pollyanna anxiously, "but I'm not to blame. And I don't think even Aunt Polly will say I am, either."

"She won't have a chance," retorted Nancy, with huge satisfaction. "She's gone."

"Gone!" gasped Pollyanna. "You don't mean that I've driven her away?"

"Not much you did," scoffed Nancy. "Her

cousin died suddenly down to Boston, and she had to go. She had one of them yellow telegram letters after you went away this afternoon, and she won't be back for three days. Now I guess we're glad all right."

"Glad! Oh, Nancy, when it's a funeral?" Pollyanna looked shocked.

"Oh, but it wasn't the funeral I was glad for, Miss Pollyanna. It was —" Nancy stopped abruptly. A shrewd twinkle came into her eyes. "Why, Miss Pollyanna, it was yourself that was teaching me to play the game."

Pollyanna puckered her forehead into a troubled frown.

"I can't help it, Nancy," she insisted with a shake of her head. "It must be that there are some things it isn't right to play the game on — and I'm sure funerals is one of them. There's nothing in a funeral to be glad about."

"We can be glad it ain't our'n," Nancy observed demurely. But Pollyanna did not hear. She had begun to tell of the accident and in a moment Nancy, open-mouthed, was listening.

Pollyanna met Jimmy Bean at the appointed place the next afternoon. As was to be expected, of course, Jimmy showed keen disappointment that the Ladies' Aid preferred a little India boy to himself.

"Well, maybe it's natural," he sighed. "Wouldn't it be just great now if somebody over in India wanted me?"

Pollyanna clapped her hands.

"Why of course! That's the very thing, Jimmy! I'll write to *my* Ladies' Aiders about you."

Jimmy's face brightened.

"Do you think they would — truly take me?" he asked.

"Of course they would! They can just play you are the little India boy this time. I'll write Mrs. White. No, I'll write Mrs. Jones. Mrs. White has got the most money, but Mrs. Jones gives the most — which is kind of funny, isn't it? But I reckon some of the Aiders will take you."

"All right — but don't forget to say I'll work for my board an' keep," put in Jimmy. "I ain't no beggar. I suppose I better stay where I am for a spell yet — till you hear."

"Of course." Pollyanna nodded emphatically. "Then I'll know just where to find you."

It was about a week after the accident in Pendleton Woods that Pollyanna said to her aunt one morning:

"Aunt Polly, would you mind very much if I took Mrs. Snow's calf's-foot jelly to someone else this week? I'm sure Mrs. Snow wouldn't mind this once."

"What are you up to now, Pollyanna?" asked her aunt. "You are the most extraordinary child!"

Pollyanna frowned a little anxiously.

"Aunt Polly, please, what is extraordinary? If you're extraordinary you can't be ordinary, can you?"

"You certainly can not."

"Oh, that's all right, then. I'm glad I'm extraordinary," said Pollyanna. "You see, Mrs. White used to say Mrs. Rawson was a very ordinary woman — and she disliked Mrs. Rawson something awful. They were always fight — I mean, Father had — that is, I mean, *we* had more trouble keeping peace between them than we did between any of the rest of the Aiders."

"Yes, well, never mind," interposed Aunt Polly, a trifle impatiently. "You do run on so, Pollyanna, and no matter what we're talking about you always bring up those Ladies' Aiders!"

"Yes'm, I reckon I do. But you see they used to bring me up, and — "

"That will do, Pollyanna," interrupted a cold voice. "Now what is it about this jelly?"

"Nothing that you would mind, Aunt Polly,

I'm sure. You let me take the jelly to her, so I thought you would to him — this once. Broken legs aren't like lifelong invalids, so his won't last forever."

"Him? He? Broken leg? What are you talking about, Pollyanna?"

Pollyanna stared, then her face relaxed.

"Oh, I forgot you didn't know. You see, it happened while you were gone. It was the very day you went that I found him in the woods. I had to unlock his house and telephone for the doctor, and hold his head, and everything. And of course then I came away and haven't seen him since. But when Nancy made the jelly for Mrs. Snow this week I thought how nice it would be if I could take it to him instead of her, just this once. Aunt Polly, may I?"

"Yes, yes, I suppose so," acquiesced Miss Polly a little wearily. "Who did you say he was?"

"Mr. John Pendleton."

Miss Polly almost sprang from her chair.

"*John Pendleton!*"

"Yes. Nancy told me his name. Maybe you know him."

Miss Polly did not answer this. Instead she asked:

"Do *you* know him?"

Pollyanna nodded.

"Oh, yes. I'll go and get the jelly. Nancy had it almost fixed when I came in," Pollyanna was already halfway across the room.

"Pollyanna, wait!" Miss Polly's voice was suddenly very stern. "I've changed my mind. I would prefer that Mrs. Snow had that jelly today — as usual. That is all. You may go now."

Pollyanna's face fell.

"Oh, but Aunt Polly, she can always be sick and have things. His is just a broken leg, and legs don't last — I mean, broken ones. He's had it a whole week now."

"Yes, I remember. I heard Mr. John Pendleton had met with an accident," said Miss Polly, a little stiffly, "but I do not care to be sending jelly to John Pendleton, Pollyanna."

"I know he is cross outside," admitted Pollyanna, "so I suppose you don't like him. But I wouldn't say it was you sent it. I'd say it was me. I like him. I'd be glad to send him jelly."

Miss Polly began to shake her head again. Then suddenly she stopped and asked in a curiously quiet voice:

"Does he know who you are, Pollyanna?"

The little girl sighed.

"I reckon not. I told him my name once, but he never calls me it — never."

"Does he know where you live?"

"Oh, no. I never told him that."

"Then he doesn't know you're my niece?"

"I don't think so."

For a moment there was silence. Miss Polly was looking at Pollyanna with eyes that did not seem to see her at all. Then Miss Polly roused herself with a start.

"Very well, Pollyanna," she said at last in that queer voice, so unlike her own, "you may take the jelly to Mr. Pendleton as your own gift. But understand: I do not send it. Be very sure that he does not think I do!"

"Yes'm. Thank you, Aunt Polly," called Pollyanna as she flew through the door.

Dr. Chilton

THE GRAY PILE of masonry looked very different to Pollyanna when she made her second visit to the house of Mr. John Pendleton. Windows were open, an elderly woman was hanging out clothes in the backyard, and the doctor's gig stood under the porte cochere.

As before Pollyanna went to the side door. This time she rang the bell.

A familiar looking small dog bounded up the steps to greet her, but there was a slight delay before the woman who had been hanging out the clothes opened the door.

"If you please, I've brought some calf's-foot jelly for Mr. Pendleton." Pollyanna smiled.

"Thank you," said the woman, reaching for the bowl in the little girl's hand. "Who shall I say sent it? And it's calf's-foot jelly?"

The doctor, coming into the hall at that moment, heard the woman's words and saw the disappointed look on Pollyanna's face. He stepped quickly forward.

"Ah! Some calf's-foot jelly?" he asked genially. "That will be fine! Maybe you'd like to see our patient, eh?"

"Oh, yes, sir," Pollyanna beamed, and the woman, in obedience to a nod from the doctor, led the way down the hall at once, though plainly with vast surprise on her face.

Behind the doctor, a young man (a trained nurse from the nearest city) gave a disturbed exclamation.

"But, Doctor, didn't Mr. Pendleton give orders not to admit anyone?"

"Oh, yes," answered the doctor, imperturbably. "But I'm giving orders now. I'll take the risk. You don't know it, of course, but that little girl is better than a six-quart bottle of tonic any day. If anything or anybody can take the grouch out of Pendleton this afternoon, she can. That's why I sent her in."

"Who is she?"

For one brief moment the doctor hesitated.

"She's the niece of one of our best-known residents. Her name is Pollyanna Whittier. I don't happen to enjoy a very extensive personal acquaintance with the little lady as yet, but lots of my patients do — I'm thankful to say!"

The nurse smiled.

"Indeed! And what are the special ingredients of the wonder-working tonic of hers?"

The doctor shook his head.

"I don't know. As near as I can find out it is an overwhelming, unquenchable gladness for everything that has happened or is going to happen. I wish I could prescribe her and buy her — as I would a box of pills."

Pollyanna, meanwhile, was being escorted to John Pendleton's rooms.

Her way led through the great library at the end of the hall, and Pollyanna saw at once that great changes had taken place. The book-lined walls and the crimson curtains were the same, but there was no litter on the floor, no untidiness on the desk, and not so much as a grain of dust in sight. The telephone card hung in its proper place and the brass andirons had been polished. One of the mysterious doors was open, and it was toward this that the maid led the way. A moment later Pollyanna found herself in a sumptuously furnished bedroom, and the maid was saying in a frightened voice:

"If you please, sir, here's a little girl with some jelly. The doctor said I was to bring her in."

The next moment Pollyanna found herself alone with a very cross-looking man lying flat on his back in bed.

"See here, didn't I say — " began an angry voice. "Oh, it's you!" Pollyanna advanced toward the bed.

"Yes, sir. I'm so glad they let me in! I was so afraid I wasn't going to see you at all. Then the doctor came and he said I might. Wasn't he lovely to let me see you?"

In spite of himself the man's lips twitched into a smile. But all he said was "Humph!"

"And I've brought you some jelly," resumed Pollyanna, "calf's-foot. I hope you like it?" There was a rising inflection in her voice.

"Never ate it." The fleeting smile had gone, and the scowl had come back to the man's face.

"Didn't you? Well, if you didn't, then you can't know you don't like it can you? So I'm glad you haven't, after all. Now, if you knew — "

"There's one thing I know all right, and that is that I'm flat on my back right here, and I'm liable to stay here till doomsday, I guess."

Pollyanna looked shocked.

"Oh, no! It couldn't be till doomsday, unless it should come quicker than we think it will."

John Pendleton laughed suddenly — and aloud. The nurse, coming in at that moment, heard the laugh, and beat a hurried retreat. He had the air of a frightened cook who, seeing the danger of a breath of cold air striking a half-done cake, hastily shuts the oven door.

Pollyanna continued to explain: "Legs don't last — broken ones, you know. Yours won't last till doomsday at all. I should think you could be glad of that."

"Oh, I am," retorted the man grimly.

"And you didn't break but one. You can be glad it wasn't two." Pollyanna was warming to her task.

"Of course! So fortunate," sniffed the man. "Looking at it from that standpoint, I suppose I might be glad I wasn't a centipede and didn't break fifty!"

Pollyanna chuckled.

"And of course," the man said sharply, all the old bitterness coming back in his voice, "I can be glad too for all the rest, I suppose — the nurse, and the doctor, and that confounded woman in the kitchen!"

"Why, yes, sir — only think how bad it would be if you *didn't* have them!"

"Well, I — eh?" he demanded sharply.

"Think how bad it would be if you didn't have them — and you lying here like this!"

"As if that isn't the very thing that's at the bottom of the whole matter," retorted the man testily. "I *am* lying here like this! Yet you expect me to say I'm glad because of a fool woman who disarranges the whole house and calls it 'regulating,' and a man who aids and abets her in it, and calls it 'nursing,' to say nothing of the doctor who eggs them both on — and the whole bunch of them, meanwhile, expecting me to pay them for it, and pay them well too!"

"Yes, I know. That part is too bad — about the money — when you've been saving it too, all this time."

"When — eh?"

"Saving it — buying beans and fish cakes. Do you like beans, or do you like turkey better?"

"Look here, child, what are you talking about?"

"About your money, you know — denying yourself, and saving it for the missionaries. You see, I found out about it. Why, Mr. Pendleton, that's one of the ways I knew you weren't cross inside. Nancy told me."

The man's jaw dropped.

"Nancy told you I was saving money for the — Well, may I inquire who Nancy is?"

"Our Nancy. She works for Aunt Polly."

"Aunt Polly! Well, who is Aunt Polly?"

"She's Miss Polly Harrington. I live with her."

The man made a sudden movement.

"Miss — Polly — Harrington!" he breathed. "You live with — *her!*"

"Yes. I'm her niece. She's taken me to bring up — on account of my mother, you know." Pollyanna's voice faltered. "She was her sister, and after Father — there wasn't anyone left for me but the Ladies' Aid, so she took me."

The man did not answer. His face, as he lay back on the pillow, was very white — so white that Pollyanna was frightened. She rose uncertainly to her feet.

"Maybe I'd better go now," she said. "I — I hope you'll like the jelly."

The man turned his head suddenly, and opened his eyes. There was a curious longing in their dark depths which even Pollyanna saw, and at which she marveled.

"So you are Miss Polly Harrington's niece," he said gently.

"Yes, sir."

Still the man's dark eyes lingered on her face. Pollyanna, feeling vaguely restless, murmured, "I suppose you know her."

John Pendleton's lip curved in an odd smile.

"Oh, yes, I know her." He hesitated, then went on, still with that curious smile. "But you don't mean — you can't mean that it was Miss Polly Harrington who sent that jelly to me?" he said slowly.

Pollyanna looked distressed.

"N-no, sir, she didn't. She said I must be very sure not to let you think she did send it. But I — "

"I thought as much," vouchsafed the man, turning his head away. Pollyanna, still more distressed, tiptoed from the room.

Under the porte cochere she found the doctor waiting in his gig. The nurse stood on the steps.

"Well, Miss Pollyanna, may I have the pleasure of seeing you home?" asked the doctor smilingly.

"Thank you, sir. I just love to ride." Pollyanna beamed as he reached out his hand to help her in.

"Do you?" The doctor nodded his head in farewell to the young man on the steps. "As near as I can judge, there are a good many things you 'love' to do," he added, as they drove briskly away.

Pollyanna laughed.

"Why, I don't know. I reckon perhaps there are," she admitted. "I like to do almost everything that's living. Of course I don't like the other things very well — sewing, and reading out loud, and all that. But they aren't living."

"No? What are they then?"

"Aunt Polly says they're learning to live," replied Pollyanna, with a rueful smile.

The doctor smiled a little queerly.

"Does she? Well, I should think she might say just that."

"Yes," responded Pollyanna. "But I don't see it that way at all. I don't think you have to learn how to live. I didn't, anyhow."

The doctor drew a long sigh.

"I'm afraid some of us do have to," he said. Then for a time he was silent. Pollyanna, stealing a glance at his face, felt vaguely sorry for him. He looked so sad. She wished, uneasily, that she could do something. It was this perhaps that caused her to say in a timid voice:

"Dr. Chilton, I should think being a doctor would be the gladdest kind of business there was."

The doctor turned in surprise.

"Gladdest — when I see so much suffering always, everywhere I go?" he cried.

She nodded.

"I know, but you're *helping* — don't you see?

The doctor's eyes filled with sudden hot tears. His life was a singularly lonely one. He had no wife and no home save his two-room office in a boarding house. His profession was very dear to him.

"God bless you," he said unsteadily.

The doctor left Pollyanna at her own door, smiled at Nancy, who was sweeping off the front porch, and drove rapidly away.

Pollyanna found her aunt in the sitting room.

"Who was that man — the one who drove into the yard, Pollyanna?" questioned the lady a little sharply.

"Why, Aunt Polly, that was Dr. Chilton! Don't you know him?"

"Dr. Chilton! What was he doing here?"

"He drove me home. Oh, and I gave the jelly to Mr. Pendleton and — "

Miss Polly lifted her head quickly.

"Pollyanna, he did not think I sent it?"

"Oh, no, Aunt Polly. I told him you didn't."

Miss Polly grew a sudden vivid pink.

"You *told* him I didn't!"

Pollyanna opened her eyes wide at the dismay in her aunt's voice.

"Why, Aunt Polly, you said to!"

"I *said*, Pollyanna, that I did not send it and for you to be very sure that he did not think I did? That is a very different matter from telling him outright that I did not send it." Aunt Polly sighed and turned vexedly away.

"Well, I don't see where the difference is," Pollyanna said to herself, as she went to hang her hat on the one particular hook on which Aunt Polly had said it must be hung.

A Red Rose
and a Lace Shawl

IT WAS ON A rainy day, about a week after
Pollyanna's visit to Mr. John Pendleton, that
Miss Polly was driven by Timothy to an early
afternoon committee meeting of the Ladies'
Aid Society. When she returned at three
o'clock, her cheeks were a bright pink and her
hair, blown by the damp wind, had fluffed into
kinks and curls wherever the pins had been
loosened.

Pollyanna had never before seen her aunt
look like this.

"You don't know how pretty you look with
your hair like that, Aunt Polly. Please, may I
do your hair like I did Mrs. Snow's. I'd so love

to see you that way! Why you'd be ever so much prettier than she was!"

"Nonsense! Pollyanna, what did you mean by going to the Ladies' Aid the other day in that absurd fashion about that beggar boy?"

Miss Polly spoke very sharply — all the more sharply because Pollyanna's words had given her an odd throb of joy. When had anybody cared how she looked? When had anybody loved to see her looking pretty? "Pollyanna, you did not answer my question. Why did you go to the Ladies' Aid in that absurd fashion?"

"Yes'm, I know. But I didn't know it was absurd until I went and found out they'd rather see their report grow than Jimmy. So then I wrote to my Ladies' Aiders. I thought maybe he could be their little India boy. Aunt Polly, was I your little India girl? And, Aunt Polly, you will let me do your hair, won't you?"

Aunt Polly put her hand to her throat. The old helpless feeling was upon her.

"But, Pollyanna, when the ladies told me this afternoon how you came to them, I — "

Pollyanna began to jump up and down on her toes.

"You didn't — you didn't say I couldn't do your hair, " she cried triumphantly. "Now wait just where you are. I'll get a comb."

"But Pollyanna," remonstrated her aunt,

following the little girl from the room and hurrying upstairs after her. "But, Pollyanna, I — I — "

Miss Polly did not finish her sentence. To her helpless amazement she found herself in the low chair before the dressing table, with her hair tumbling about her ears.

"Oh, what pretty hair you've got," exclaimed Pollyanna.

"Pollyanna, I'm sure I don't know why I'm letting you do this silly thing."

"Why, Aunt Polly, I should think you'd be glad to have folks like to look at you! Don't you like to look at pretty things?"

"But — but — "

"And I just love to do folks' hair," purred Pollyanna, contentedly. "I did quite a lot of the Ladies' Aiders' — but there weren't any of them so nice as yours. Oh, Aunt Polly, I just happened to think of something! But it's a secret and I won't tell. I'm going to leave you just a minute, and you must promise not to peek at your hair till I come back. Now remember!" she finished, as she ran from the room.

Aloud Miss Polly said nothing. To herself she said that she should undo the absurd work and put her hair up properly again. As for peeking — just as if she cared how —

At that moment Miss Polly caught a glimpse

of herself in the mirror of the dressing table. What she saw sent a flush of rosy color to her cheeks.

She saw a face — not young, it is true — but alight with excitement and surprise. The cheeks were a pretty pink. The eyes sparkled. The hair, dark and still damp from the outdoor air, lay in loose waves about the forehead with softening curls here and there.

So amazed and absorbed was Miss Polly with what she saw in the glass that she forgot her determination to do her hair over until she heard Pollyanna enter the room again. Before she could move, she felt something slipped across her eyes.

"Pollyanna! Pollyanna! What are you doing?" she cried.

Pollyanna chuckled.

"That's just what I don't want you to know, Aunt Polly. That's why I tied on the handkerchief. Now sit still. It won't take a minute, then I'll let you see."

"But, Pollyanna," began Miss Polly, struggling blindly to her feet, "you must take this off! What *are* you doing?" she gasped, as she felt something soft slipped about her shoulders.

Pollyanna was draping the fleecy folds of a beautiful lace shawl, yellowed from long years of packing away and fragrant with lavender, about her aunt's shoulders. Pollyanna had found the shawl the week before when Nancy had been straightening the attic.

Her task completed, Pollyanna surveyed her work. But she saw yet one touch wanting. Promptly, she pulled her aunt toward the sun parlor, where she could see a red rose blooming on the trellis within reach of her hand.

"Pollyanna, what are you doing? Where are you taking me?" Aunt Polly recoiled, vainly trying to hold herself back. "Pollyanna, I shall not — "

"It's just to the sun parlor. Only a minute and I'll have you ready now in no time," said Pollyanna, reaching for the rose and thrusting it into the soft hair above Miss Polly's left ear. "There!" she exulted, untying the knot of the handkerchief and flinging the bit of linen far from her. "Oh, Aunt Polly, now I reckon you'll be glad I dressed you up!"

For one dazed moment Miss Polly looked at herself and at her surroundings, then she gave a low cry and fled to her room. Pollyanna, following the direction of her aunt's dismayed gaze, saw a horse and gig turning into the driveway. She recognized the man who held the rains at once.

Delightedly she leaned through the open windows of the sun parlor.

"Dr. Chilton, Dr. Chilton!" she called. "Did you want to see me? I'm up here."

"Yes," replied the doctor, a little gravely. "Will you come down, please?"

In her bedroom, Pollyanna found a flushed-faced, angry-eyed Aunt Polly plucking at the pins that held the lace shawl in place.

"Pollyanna, how could you?" moaned Aunt Polly. "To think of rigging me up like this and letting me be seen!"

Pollyanna stared in dismay.

"But you looked lovely, Aunt Polly, and — "

" 'Lovely'!" scorned the woman, flinging the shawl to one side and attacking her hair with shaking fingers.

"Oh, Aunt Polly, please, please let the hair stay!"

"Stay? Like this? As if I would!" Miss Polly pulled her hair back so tightly that the curls lay stretched dead at the ends of her fingers.

"Oh dear! And you did look so pretty." Pollyanna almost sobbed as she stumbled through the door.

Downstairs Pollyanna found the doctor waiting in his gig.

"I've prescribed you for a patient, and he's sent me to get the prescription filled," announced the doctor. "Will you go?"

"You mean an errand to the drug store?"

asked Pollyanna, a little uncertainly.

The doctor shook his head with a smile.

"Not exactly. It's Mr. Pendleton. He would like to see you today, if you'll be so good as to come. Will you come? I'll call for you and bring you back before six o'clock."

"I'd love to!" exclaimed Pollyanna. "Let me ask Aunt Polly."

In a few moments she returned, hat in hand, but with rather a sober face.

"Didn't your aunt want you to go?" the doctor asked, as they drove away.

"Yes," sighed Pollyanna. "She wanted me to go too much, I'm afraid."

"Wanted you to go *too much!*"

Pollyanna sighed again. "Yes. I reckon she meant she didn't want me there. She said: 'Yes, yes, run along, run along — do! I wish you'd gone before.'"

The doctor's eyes were very grave. For some time he said nothing, then, a little hesitatingly, he asked:

"Wasn't it your aunt I saw with you a few minutes ago in the window of the sun parlor?"

Pollyanna drew a long breath.

"Yes, that was the whole trouble, I suppose. You see I dressed her up in a lovely lace shawl I found upstairs, and fixed her hair and put in a rose, and she looked so pretty. Didn't you think she looked lovely?"

For a moment the doctor did not answer. When he did speak his voice was so low Pollyanna could just hear the words.

"Yes, Pollyanna. I thought she did look lovely."

"I'm so glad. I'll tell her," said the little girl, contentedly.

To her surprise the doctor gave a sudden exclamation.

"No, Pollyanna, I'm afraid I shall have to ask you not to tell her that."

"Why, Dr. Chilton! Why not? I should think you'd be glad — "

"But she might not be," cut in the doctor.

Pollyanna considered this for a moment.

"That's so. Maybe she wouldn't," she agreed. "I remember now, it was because she saw you that she ran. And she spoke about being seen in that rig."

"I thought as much," declared the doctor, under his breath.

"Still, I don't see why," maintained Pollyanna, "when she looked so pretty!"

The doctor said nothing. He did not speak again until they were almost to the great stone house in which John Pendleton lay with a broken leg.

"Just Like a Book"

JOHN PENDLETON GREETED Pollyanna with a smile. "Well, Miss Pollyanna, you must be a very forgiving little person, else you wouldn't have come to see me again today."

"Why, Mr. Pendleton, I was real glad to come, and I don't see why I shouldn't be, either."

"Oh, well, you know, I was pretty cross with you the other day when you so kindly brought me the jelly, and that first time when you found me with the broken leg. By the way, I don't think I've ever thanked you for that. Now I'm sure that even you would admit that you were very forgiving to come and see me, after such ungrateful treatment as that!"

Pollyanna stirred uneasily.

"But I was glad to find you. I don't mean I was glad your leg was broken, of course," she corrected hurriedly.

John Pendleton smiled.

"I understand. Your tongue does get away with you once in a while, doesn't it, Miss Pollyanna? I consider you a very brave little girl to do what you did that day. I thank you for the jelly too," he added in a lighter voice.

"Did you like it?" asked Pollyanna.

"Very much. I suppose there isn't any more today that Aunt Polly didn't send, is there?" he asked with a smile.

His visitor looked distressed.

"N-no sir." She hesitated, then went on with heightened color. "Please, Mr. Pendleton, I didn't mean to be rude the other day when I said Aunt Polly did not send the jelly."

There was no answer. John Pendleton was not smiling now. He was looking straight ahead of him with eyes that seemed to be gazing through and beyond the objects before them. After a time he drew a long sigh and turned to Pollyanna. When he spoke his voice carried the old nervous fretfulness.

"This will never do! I didn't send for you to see me moping this time. Listen. Out in the library you will find a carved box on the lower shelf of the big case with glass doors. You may bring it to me. It is not too heavy for you to carry, I think."

"Oh, I'm awfully strong," declared Pollyanna, cheerfully, as she sprang to her feet. In a minute she had returned with the box.

It was a wonderful half-hour that Pollyanna spent then. The box was full of treasures — curios that John Pendleton had picked up in years of travel. Concerning each one there was some entertaining story, whether it was a set of exquisitely carved chessmen from China, or a little jade idol from India.

It was after she had heard the story about the idol that Pollyanna murmured wistfully:

"I suppose it would be better to bring up a little boy in India — still I can't help wishing they had wanted Jimmy Bean too."

John Pendleton did not seem to hear. His eyes were staring straight before him, looking at nothing. But soon he had roused himself, and had picked up another curio to talk about.

Before the visit was over, they were talking of Nancy, of Aunt Polly, and of Pollyanna's daily life. They were talking too of her life and home long ago.

"Pollyanna, I want you to come and see me often. Will you? I'm lonesome, but there's another reason — and I'm going to tell you that too. I thought at first, after I found out who you were, that I didn't want you to come anymore. You reminded me of something I have tried for years to forget. I said to myself that I never wanted to see you again, and every day, when the doctor asked if I wouldn't let him bring you to me, I said no.

"But after a time I found that the fact that I wasn't seeing you was making me remember all the more vividly the thing I was wanting to forget. So now I want you to come. Will you?"

"Why, yes, Mr. Pendleton," Pollyanna's eyes were luminous with sympathy for the sad-faced man lying back on the pillow before her. "I'd love to come!"

"Thank you," said John Pendleton, gently.

After supper that evening, Pollyanna, sitting on the back porch, told Nancy all about Mr. John Pendleton's wonderful carved box and the still more wonderful things it contained.

"But what beats me is how he happened to take to you, Miss Pollyanna — meaning no offense to you, of course. But he ain't the sort of man what generally takes to kids."

Pollyanna smiled happily. "But he did, Nancy. Only I reckon he didn't want to. Why only today he owned up that one time he never wanted to see me again because I reminded him of something he wanted to forget. But afterward — "

"What's that?" interrupted Nancy, excitedly. "He said you reminded him of something he wanted to forget?"

"Yes. But afterward — "

"What was it?" Nancy was eagerly insistent.

"He didn't tell me. He just said it was something."

"The mystery!" breathed Nancy, in an awestruck voice. "That's why he took to you in the first place. Oh, Miss Pollyanna! Why, that's just like a book. I've read lots of 'em, *Lady Maud's Secret* and *The Lost Heir* and *Hidden for Years* — all of 'em had mysteries and things just like this. My stars and stockings! Just think of having a book lived right under your nose like this. Now tell me everything — everything he said, Miss Pollyanna, there's a dear! No wonder he took to you. No wonder — no wonder!"

"But he didn't," cried Pollyanna, "not till I told him first. He didn't even know who I was till I took the calf's-foot jelly, and had to make him understand that Aunt Polly didn't send it, and — "

Nancy sprang to her feet and clasped her hands together.

"Oh, Miss Pollyanna, I know, I know —

I *know* I know! she cried rapturously. The next minute she was down at Pollyanna's side again. "Tell me — now think, and answer straight and true," she urged excitedly. "It was after he found out you was Miss Polly's niece that he said he didn't ever want to see you again, wasn't it?"

"Yes. That's what he told me today."

"I thought as much," triumphed Nancy. "And Miss Polly wouldn't send the jelly herself, would she?"

"No."

"And you told him she didn't send it?"

"Why, yes, I — "

"And he began to act queer and cry out sudden after he found out you was her niece. He did that, didn't he?"

"Why, yes. He did act a little queer," admitted Pollyanna, with a thoughtful frown.

Nancy drew a long sigh.

"Then I've got it, sure! Now listen. Mr. John Pendleton was in love with Miss Polly Harrington," she announced impressively, but with a furtive glance over her shoulder.

"Why, Nancy, he couldn't be. She doesn't like him," objected Pollyanna.

Nancy gave her a scornful glance.

"Of course she don't! *That's* the quarrel!"

Pollyanna still looked incredulous, and with

another long breath Nancy happily settled herself to tell the story.

"It's like this. Just before you come, Mr. Tom told me Miss Polly had been in love. I didn't believe it. I couldn't — her in love! But Mr. Tom said she had, and that the feller was living right now in this town. And now I know, of course. It's John Pendleton. Ain't he got a mystery in his life? Don't he shut himself up in that grand house alone and never speak to no one? Didn't he act queer when he found out you was Miss Polly's niece? And now ain't he owned up that you remind him of something he wants to forget? Just as if anybody couldn't see it was Miss Polly! Why, Miss Pollyanna, it's as plain as the nose on your face."

"Oh-h!" breathed Pollyanna, in wide-eyed amazement. "But, Nancy, I should think if they loved each other they'd make up some time. Both of 'em so all alone all these years. I should think they'd be glad to make up!"

Nancy sniffed disdainfully.

"I guess maybe you don't know much about being in love, Miss Pollyanna. You ain't big enough yet, anyhow. But if there is a set of folks in the world that wouldn't have no use for that glad game of your'n, it would be a pair of quarreling lovers, and that's what they be. Ain't he cross as sticks, most generally? — and ain't she — "

Nancy stopped, remembering just in time to whom, and about whom, she was speaking. Then, she continued.

"I ain't saying, though, Miss Pollyanna, but it would be a pretty slick piece of business if you could get 'em to make up. But, my land! wouldn't folks stare some — Miss Polly and him! I guess though there ain't much chance."

Pollyanna said nothing. But when she went into the house a little later, her face was very thoughtful.

Prisms

As the warm August days passed, Pollyanna
went frequently to the great house on Pendleton Hill. She did not feel, however, that her
visits were really a success. The man seemed
to want her there, but when she was there, he
seemed scarcely any the happier for her presence — at least so Pollyanna thought.

He talked to her, it was true, but she was
never sure she would not look up and see that
white, hurt look that always pained her.
And she was never sure which — if any — of
her words had brought it there. As for telling
him the "glad game," Pollyanna had never
seen the time yet when he would care to hear

about it. She had tried twice to tell him, but neither time had she got beyond the beginning of what her father had said. On each occasion John Pendleton had turned the conversation abruptly to another subject.

Pollyanna never doubted now that John Pendleton was in love with her Aunt Polly. And with all the strength of her loving, loyal heart, she wished she could in some way bring happiness into their miserably lonely lives.

Just how she was to do this, she could not see. She talked to Mr. Pendleton about her aunt, and he listened, sometimes politely, sometimes irritably. She talked to her aunt about Mr. Pendleton, or rather she tried to talk to her about him. As a general thing, however, Miss Polly would not listen. She always found something else to talk about. She frequently did that, however, when Pollyanna was talking of others — of Dr. Chilton, for instance. Pollyanna laid this to the fact that it had been Dr. Chilton who had seen her in the sun parlor with the rose in her hair and the lace shawl draped about her shoulders. Aunt Polly, in fact, seemed particularly bitter against Dr. Chilton, as Pollyanna found out one day when a bad cold shut her up in the house.

"If you are not better by night I shall send for the doctor," Aunt Polly said.

"Shall you? Then I'm going to be worse,"

teased Pollyanna. "I'd love to have Dr. Chilton come to see me!"

"It will not be Dr. Chilton, Pollyanna," Miss Polly said sternly. "Dr. Chilton is not our family physician. I shall send for Dr. Warren — if you are worse."

Pollyanna did not grow worse, however, and Dr. Warren was not summoned.

"I'm glad too," Pollyanna said to her aunt that evening. "Of course I like Dr. Warren, but I like Dr. Chilton better, and I'm afraid he'd feel hurt if I didn't have him. He wasn't to blame after all because he happened to see you when I dressed you up so pretty that day, Aunt Polly," she finished wistfully.

"That will do, Pollyanna. I do not wish to discuss Dr. Chilton or his feelings," reproved Miss Polly.

Pollyanna looked at her aunt for a moment with mournfully interested eyes, then she sighed.

It was toward the end of August that Pollyanna, making an early morning call on John Pendleton, found the flaming band of color lying across his pillow. She stopped short in awed delight.

"Why, Mr. Pendleton, it's a rainbow — a real rainbow," she exclaimed. "Oh, how pretty! But how did it get in?" she cried.

John Pendleton laughed a little grimly. He was particularly out of sorts with the world this morning.

"Well, I suppose it got in through the beveled edge of that glass thermometer in the window," he said wearily. "The sun shouldn't strike it at all — but it does in the morning."

"Oh, but it's so pretty, Mr. Pendleton! And does just the sun do that? If it was mine, I'd have it hang in the sun all day long!"

"Lots of good you'd get out of the thermometer then," laughed the man. "How do you suppose you could tell how hot it was or how cold it was, if the thermometer hung in the sun all day?"

"I shouldn't care," replied Pollyanna, her fascinated eyes on the brilliant band of colors across the pillow.

The man laughed. He was watching Pollyanna's face a little curiously. Suddenly he touched a bell at his side.

"Nora," he said, when the elderly maid appeared at the door, "bring me one of the big brass candlesticks from the mantel in the front drawing room."

"Yes, sir," murmured the woman, looking slightly puzzled. In a minute she had returned. A musical tinkling entered the room with her. It came from the prism pendants encircling the old-fashioned candelabrum in her hand.

"Thank you. You may set it here on the stand," directed Mr. Pendleton. "Now get a string and fasten it to the curtain fixtures on that window. Take the curtain down first. Thank you," he said, when Nora had carried out his instructions.

"Bring me the candlestick, please, Pollyanna." With both hands she carried it, and in a moment Mr. Pendleton was slipping off the pendants, until a round dozen of them lay side by side on the bed.

"Now, my dear, suppose you take them and hook them to that little string Nora fixed across the window.

Pollyanna had not hung up three of the pendants in the sunlit window before she saw a little of what was going to happen. When her task was finished, she stepped back with a cry of delight.

That sumptuous dreary bedroom had become a fairyland. Everywhere were bits of dancing red and green, violet and orange, gold and blue. The wall, the floor, and the furniture, even the bed itself, were aflame with shimmering bits of color.

"How lovely!" breathed Pollyanna. "Oh, how I wish I had a lot of those things! I would give them to Aunt Polly and Mrs. Snow and — lots of folks. I reckon then they'd be glad all right! Why, I think even Aunt Polly would get so glad she couldn't help banging doors — don't you?"

Mr. Pendleton laughed.

"From my remembrance of your aunt, Miss Pollyanna, I think it would take more than a few prisms in the sunlight to make her bang many doors. But come now, what do you mean?"

Pollyanna drew a long breath.

"I forgot. You don't know about the game."

"Suppose you tell me then."

And this time Pollyanna told him. As she talked her eyes were still on the dancing flecks of color from the prism pendants swaying in the sunlit window.

"And that's all," she nodded when she had finished.

For a moment there was silence. Then a low voice from the bed said unsteadily:

"I'm thinking the very finest prism of them all is yourself, Pollyanna."

"No," she said. "I don't show beautiful red and green and purple when the sun shines through me. I'm afraid the sun doesn't make anything but freckles out of me."

The man laughed a little, and Pollyanna turned to look at him: The laugh sounded almost like a sob.

Which Is Somewhat Surprising

Pollyanna entered school in September. She passed the preliminary examinations, and was soon a happy member of a class of girls and boys her own age.

School, in some ways, was a surprise to Pollyanna. And Pollyanna, in many ways, was a surprise to school. They were soon on the best of terms, however, and Pollyanna confessed to her aunt that going to school was living after all — though she had had her doubts before.

In spite of her delight in her new work, Pollyanna did not forget her old friends. True, she could not give them quite so much time now, but she gave them what time she could.

John Pendleton was the most dissatisfied. One Saturday afternoon he spoke to her about it.

"See here, Pollyanna, how would you like to come and live with me?" he asked. "I don't see anything of you, nowadays."

"I thought you didn't like to have folks around," she said.

He made a wry face.

"Oh, but that was before you taught me to play that game of yours. Now I'm glad to be waited on hand and foot," he said, picking up one of the crutches at his side and shaking it playfully at Pollyanna. They were sitting in the great library.

"Oh, but you aren't really glad at all for things, you just say you are." Pollyanna pouted, her eyes on the dog dozing before the fire. "You know you don't play the game right, Mr. Pendleton — you know you don't!"

The man's face grew suddenly very grave.

"That's why I want you to live here — to help me play it. Will you come?"

Pollyanna turned in surprise.

"Mr. Pendleton, you don't really mean that?"

"But I do. Will you come?"

Pollyanna looked distressed.

"Why, Mr. Pendleton, I can't. You know I can't. Why, I'm Aunt Polly's!"

An expression crossed the man's face that Pollyanna could not quite understand. His head came up almost fiercely.

"You're no more hers than — Perhaps she would let you come to me," he finished more gently. "Would you come if she did?"

Pollyanna frowned in deep thought.

"But Aunt Polly has been so good to me," she began slowly. "She took me when I didn't have anybody but the Ladies' Aid."

Mr. Pendleton's voice was low and very sad.

"Pollyanna, long years ago, I loved somebody very much. I hoped some day to bring her to this house. I pictured how happy we'd be together in our home in all the long years to come."

"Yes," Pollyanna's eyes were shining with interest.

"But — well, I didn't bring her here. Never mind why. I just didn't — that's all. Ever since then this great gray pile of stone has been a house, never a home. It takes a woman's hand and heart or a child's presence to make a home, Pollyanna, and I have not had either. Now will you come, my dear?"

Pollyanna sprang to her feet. Her face was beaming.

"Mr. Pendleton, you mean that you wish you

had that woman's hand and heart all this time?"

"Why, y-yes, Pollyanna."

"Oh, I'm so glad! Then it's all right," said the little girl. "Now you can take us both."

"Take you both?" asked the man dazedly.

A faint doubt crossed Pollyanna's countenance.

"Well, of course Aunt Polly isn't won over yet, but I'm sure she will be if you talk to her just as you did to me. Then we'd both come."

A look of actual terror leaped to the man's eyes.

"Aunt Polly — come here!"

Pollyanna's eyes widened a little.

"Would you rather go there?" she asked. "Of course, the house isn't so pretty, but it's nearer to — "

"Pollyanna, what are you talking about?" asked the man, very gently now.

"About where we're going to live of course," rejoined Pollyanna, in obvious surprise. "You said it was here that you wanted Aunt Polly's hand and heart all these years and — "

An inarticulate cry came from the man's throat. He raised his hand and began to speak, but the next moment he dropped his hand at his side.

"The doctor, sir," said the maid in the doorway.

Pollyanna rose at once.

John Pendleton turned to her quickly.

"Pollyanna, for Heaven's sake, say nothing of what I asked you — yet," he begged in a low voice.

"Of course not! As if I didn't know you'd rather tell her yourself," Pollyanna called back over her shoulder.

John Pendleton fell back limply in his chair.

"What's up?" demanded the doctor a minute later, his fingers on his patient's galloping pulse.

A whimsical smile trembled on John Pendleton's lips.

"Overdose of your tonic, I guess." He laughed as he noticed the doctor watching Pollyanna go down the driveway.

Which Is More Surprising

Sunday mornings Pollyanna usually attended church and Sunday school. Sunday afternoons she frequently went for a walk with Nancy. She had planned a walk for the day after her Saturday afternoon visit to John Pendleton, but on the way home from Sunday school Dr. Chilton overtook her in his gig and brought his horse to a stop.

"Suppose you let me drive you home, Pollyanna," he said. "I want to speak to you a minute. I was just driving out to your place," he explained, as Pollyanna settled herself at his side. "Mr. Pendleton sent a special request for you to go to see him this afternoon. He says it's very important."

Pollyanna nodded happily.

"Yes it is. I know. I'll go."

The doctor eyed her with some surprise.

"I'm not sure I should let you," he declared, his eyes twinkling. "You seemed more upsetting than soothing yesterday, young lady."

"Oh, it wasn't me, not really. Not so much as it was Aunt Polly."

The doctor turned with a quick start.

"Your aunt!" he exclaimed.

Pollyanna gave a happy bounce in her seat.

"Yes. And it's so exciting, just like a story. I'm going to tell you," she burst out, with sudden decision. "He said not to mention it, but he wouldn't mind your knowing. He meant not to mention it to her."

"Her?"

"Yes, Aunt Polly. And of course he would want to tell her himself. That's the story part, you see. I didn't know it till Nancy told me. She said Aunt Polly had been in love years ago, and had quarreled. She didn't know who the man was at first. But we've found out now. It's Mr. Pendleton."

The doctor relaxed suddenly. The hand holding the reins fell limply to his lap.

"Oh! I didn't know," he said quietly.

Pollyanna hurried on — they were nearing the Harrington homestead.

"Yes, and I'm so glad now. Mr. Pendleton asked me to come and live with him, but of course I wouldn't leave Aunt Polly, she's been so good to me. But of course if he wants to make up the quarrel, everything will be all right and Aunt Polly and I will both go to live there, or else he'll come to live with us. Of course Aunt Polly doesn't know yet, and we haven't got everything settled, so I suppose that is why he wanted to see me this afternoon."

The doctor sat suddenly erect. There was an odd smile on his lips.

"Yes, I can well imagine that Mr. John Pendleton wants to see you, Pollyanna," he said as he pulled his horse to a stop before the door.

"There's Aunt Polly now, in the window," cried Pollyanna. "Why, no, she isn't — but I thought I saw her!"

"No, she isn't there now," said the doctor. His lips had suddenly lost their smile.

Pollyanna found a very nervous John Pendleton waiting for her that afternoon.

"Pollyanna," he began at once. "I've been trying all night to puzzle out what you meant yesterday about my wanting your Aunt Polly's hand and heart here all these years. What did you mean?"

"Why, because you were both in love once,

and I was so glad you still felt that way now."

"In love! — your Aunt Polly and I?"

At the obvious surprise in the man's voice, Pollyanna opened her eyes wide.

"Why, Mr. Pendleton, Nancy said you were!"

The man gave a short little laugh.

"Indeed! Well, I'm afraid I shall have to say that Nancy didn't know."

"Then you weren't?" Pollyanna's voice was tragic with dismay.

"Never!"

"And it isn't all coming out like a book?"

There was no answer. The man's eyes were moodily fixed out the window.

"Oh dear! It was all going so splendidly." Pollyanna almost sobbed. "I would have been so glad to come — with Aunt Polly."

"And you won't now?" The man asked the question without turning his head.

"Of course not! I'm Aunt Polly's."

The man turned, almost fiercely.

"Before you were hers, Pollyanna, you were your mother's. And it was your mother's hand and heart that I wanted long years ago."

"*My mother's!*"

"Yes. I had not meant to tell you, but perhaps it's better that I do." John Pendleton's face had grown very pale. He was speaking with evident difficulty. Pollyanna was gazing at him fixedly. "I loved your mother, but she didn't love me. And after a time she went away with your father. I didn't know until then how much I did care. For long years I have been a cross, crabbed, unlovable, unloved old man. Then one day, like one of the prisms that you love so much, you danced into my life. When I found out who you were, I thought I never wanted to see you again. I didn't want to be reminded of your mother. But you know how that came out. Pollyanna, won't you come — *now*?"

"But, Mr. Pendleton, there's Aunt Polly!" Pollyanna's eyes were blurred with tears.

The man made an impatient gesture.

"What about me? Pollyanna, it's only since you came that I've been even half glad to live! If I had you for my own little girl, I'd be glad for anything and I'd try to make you glad too. You shouldn't have a wish ungratified. All my money, to the last cent, should go to make you happy."

"You don't need me to make you glad about things. You're making other folks so glad giving them things that you just can't help being glad yourself! Why, look at those prisms you gave Mrs. Snow and me, and the gold piece you gave Nancy on her birthday, and — "

"Yes, yes — never mind about that," interrupted the man. His face was very red now, and no wonder, for it was not for giving things that John Pendleton had been best known in the past.

"It wasn't much, anyhow, but what there was, was because of you. You gave those things, not me! Yes, you did," he repeated, in answer to the denial in her face. "And that only goes to prove all the more how I need you," he added.

"Aunt Polly has been so good to me," Pollyanna began to explain, but the man interrupted her sharply.

"Of course she's been good to you! But she doesn't want you, half so much as I do," he contested.

"Why, Mr. Pendleton, she's glad to have — "

"Glad!" interrupted the man, thoroughly losing his patience now. "I'll wager Miss Polly doesn't know how to be glad — for anything! Oh, she does her duty, I know. She's a very dutiful woman. I'll acknowledge we haven't been the best of friends for the last fifteen or twenty years, but I know her. Everyone knows her — and she isn't the glad kind, Pollyanna. She doesn't know how to be. As for your coming to me — you just ask her and see if she won't let you come."

Pollyanna rose to her feet.

"All right. I'll ask her," she said determinedly. There was a moment's silence, then she added: "Well, anyhow, I'm glad I didn't tell her yesterday."

John Pendleton smiled grimly.

"Yes, I guess it is just as well you didn't mention it yesterday."

"Only to the doctor, of course, but he doesn't count."

"The doctor!" cried John Pendleton, turning quickly. "Not Dr. Chilton?"

"Yes, when he came to tell me you wanted to see me."

"And what did Dr. Chilton say?" he asked.

"Not much. Oh, he did say he could well imagine that you wanted to see me."

"Oh, did he, indeed!" answered John Pendleton. And Pollyanna wondered why he gave that sudden queer little laugh.

A Question Answered

THE SKY WAS darkening fast with what appeared to be an approaching thunder shower when Pollyanna hurried down the hill from John Pendleton's house. Halfway home she met Nancy coming to meet her with an umbrella. By that time, however, the clouds had shifted and the shower was not so imminent.

"Guess it's going around to the north," announced Nancy, eyeing the sky critically. "I thought it was all the time, but Miss Polly wanted me to come with this. She was worried about you!"

"Was she?" murmured Pollyanna abstractedly.

"You don't seem to notice what I said," Nancy observed aggrievedly. "I said your aunt was *worried* about you!"

Pollyanna sighed, remembering the question she was so soon to ask her aunt. "I'm sorry. I didn't mean to scare her."

"Well, I'm glad," retorted Nancy, unexpectedly.

Pollyanna stared.

"Glad that Aunt Polly was scared about me! Why, Nancy, that isn't the way to play the game — to be glad for things like that!" she objected.

"There wasn't no game in it," replied Nancy. "Never thought of it. You don't seem to sense what it means to have Miss Polly worried about you."

"It means worried, and worried is horrid to feel," maintained Pollyanna. "What else can it mean?"

Nancy tossed her head.

"I'll tell you what it means. It means she's at last getting down somewhere near human, and she ain't just doing her duty by you all the time."

"Why, Nancy, Aunt Polly always does her duty. She's a very dutiful woman!" Unconsciously Pollyanna repeated John Pendleton's words.

Nancy chuckled.

"You're right she is — and she always was, I guess! But she's something more since you came."

Pollyanna's face changed. Her brows drew into a troubled frown.

"That's what I was going to ask you, Nancy. Do you think Aunt Polly likes to have me here? Would she mind if I wasn't here anymore?"

Nancy threw a quick look into the little girl's absorbed face. She had expected to be asked this question long before, and she had dreaded it. She had wondered how she could answer it honestly without cruelly hurting the questioner. But now, Nancy welcomed the question with open arms. She was sure she could set the love-hungry little girl's heart at rest.

"Likes to have you here? Would she miss you if you wasn't here?" cried Nancy, indignantly. "As if that wasn't just what I was telling you! Didn't she send me with an umbrella 'cause she saw a little cloud in the sky? Didn't she make me tote all your things downstairs so you could have the pretty room you wanted? Why, Miss Pollyanna, when you remember how at first she hated to have — "

With a choking cough Nancy pulled herself up just in time.

"And it ain't just things I can put my finger on, neither," Nancy rushed on breathlessly. "It's little ways she has, that show how you've been softening her up an' mellowing her down — the cat and the dog, and the way she speaks to me, and — oh, lots of things. Why, Miss Pollyanna, there ain't no telling how she'd miss you if you wasn't here."

"Oh, Nancy, I'm so glad! You don't know how glad I am that Aunt Polly wants me!"

"As if I'd leave her now!" thought Pollyanna, as she climbed the stairs to her room a little later. "I always knew I wanted to live with Aunt Polly, but I reckon maybe I didn't know quite how much I wanted Aunt Polly to want to live with *me*!"

The task of telling John Pendleton of her decision would not be an easy one. Pollyanna dreaded it. She was very fond of John Pendleton and she was very sorry for him — because he seemed to be so sorry for himself. She was sorry too for the long, lonely life that had made him so unhappy, and she was grieved that it had been because of her mother that he had spent those dreary years.

She pictured the great gray house as it would be after its master was well again: its silent rooms, its littered floors, its disordered desk, and her heart ached for his loneliness. She wished that somewhere, someone might be found who — It was at this point that she sprang to her feet with a cry of joy at the thought that had come to her.

As soon as she could, after that, she hurried up the hill to John Pendleton's house. In due time she found herself in the great dim library with John Pendleton sitting near her, his long thin hands lying idle on the arms of his chair and his faithful little dog at his feet.

"Well, Pollyanna?" asked the man gently.

"I've thought of the very gladdest thing for you to do."

"For me to do," repeated John Pendleton, his mouth growing a little stern at the corners. "Did she refuse to let you come?"

"I — I didn't ask her," stammered the little girl miserably.

"Pollyanna!"

Pollyanna turned away her eyes. She could not meet the hurt, grieved gaze of her friend.

"So you didn't even ask her!"

"I couldn't, sir, truly," faltered Pollyanna. "You see, I found out — without asking — that Aunt Polly wants me with her, and I want to stay too," she confessed bravely. "You don't know how good she's been to me, and I think she's beginning to be glad about things — lots of things. And you know she never used to be. You said it yourself. Oh, Mr. Pendleton, I couldn't leave Aunt Polly now!"

There was a long pause. Only the snapping of the wood fire in the grate broke the silence. At last, however, the man spoke.

"No, Pollyanna, I see. You couldn't leave her now," he said. "I won't ask you again." The last word was so low it was almost inaudible, but Pollyanna heard.

"Oh, but you don't know about the rest of it," she told him eagerly. "There's the very gladdest thing you can do!"

"Not for me, Pollyanna."

"Yes, for you. You said only a woman's hand and heart or a child's presence could make a home. And I can get it for you — a child's presence. Not me, but another one."

"As if I would have any but you!" resented an indignant voice.

"But you will when you know. You're so kind and good! Why, think of the prisms and the gold pieces, and all that money you save for the missionaries, and — "

"Pollyanna!" interrupted the man savagely. "Once and for all let us end that nonsense! I've tried to tell you half a dozen times before. There is no money for the missionaries. I never sent a penny to them in my life. There!"

He lifted his chin and braced himself to meet the grieved disappointment in Pollyanna's

.yes. To his amazement, however, there was neither grief nor disappointment. There was only surprised joy.

"Oh!" she cried, clapping her hands. "I'm so glad! I don't mean that I'm not sorry for them, only I can't help being glad that you don't want the little India boys, because now I know you'll take him!"

"Take who?"

"Jimmy Bean. I had to tell him last week that even my Ladies' Aid out west wouldn't take him, and he was so disappointed. But now when he hears of this he'll be so glad!"

"Will he? Well, I won't," said the man decisively. "Pollyanna, this is sheer nonsense!"

"You don't mean you won't take him?"

"I certainly do mean just that."

"But he'd be a lovely child's presence." Pollyanna was almost crying now. "And you couldn't be lonesome with Jimmy around."

"I don't doubt it," rejoined the man, "but I think I prefer the lonesomeness."

It was then that Pollyanna suddenly remembered something Nancy had said. She raised her chin aggrievedly.

"You think a nice live boy wouldn't be better than an old dead skeleton, but I think it would!"

"*Skeleton?*"

"Yes. Nancy said you had one in your closet somewhere."

"What — " Suddenly the man threw back his head and laughed. He laughed so heartily that Pollyanna began to cry from pure nervousness. When he saw that, his face grew grave at once.

"Pollyanna, I suspect you are right — more right than you know," he said gently. "In fact, I know that a nice live boy would be far better than any skeleton in the closet, only we aren't always willing to make the exchange. We are apt to still cling to our skeletons, Pollyanna. However, suppose you tell me a little more about this boy." And Pollyanna told him.

Perhaps the laugh cleared the air, or perhaps the pathos of Jimmy Bean's story, as told by Pollyanna, touched a heart already strangely softened. At all events, when Pollyanna went home that night she carried with her an invitation for Jimmy Bean to call at the great house with Pollyanna the next Saturday afternoon.

"And I'm so glad, and I'm sure you'll like him," said Pollyanna, as she said good-by. "I do so want Jimmy Bean to have a home — and folks that care."

An Accident

A t Mrs. Snow's request, Pollyanna went one day to Dr. Chilton's office to get the name of a medicine which Mrs. Snow had forgotten. Pollyanna had never before seen the inside of Dr. Chilton's office.

"This is your home, isn't it?" she said, looking about her.

The doctor smiled a little sadly.

"Yes — such as it is," he answered, as he wrote on the pad of paper in his hand. "It's a pretty poor apology for a home, Pollyanna. They're just rooms, that's all — not a home."

Pollyanna nodded her head wisely. Her eyes glowed with sympathetic understanding.

"I know. It takes a woman's hand and heart or a child's presence to make a home," she said.

"Eh?" The doctor wheeled about abruptly.

"Mr. Pendleton told me," explained Pollyanna. "Why don't you get a woman's hand and heart, Dr. Chilton? Or maybe you'd take Jimmy Bean if Mr. Pendleton doesn't want him."

Dr. Chilton's laugh was a little constrained.

"So Mr. Pendleton says it takes a woman's hand and heart to make a home, does he?"

"Yes. He says his is just a house too. Why don't you, Dr. Chilton?"

"Why don't I what?" The doctor had turned back to his desk.

"Get a woman's hand and heart. Oh — " Pollyanna's face suddenly showed a painful color. "I suppose I ought to tell you. It wasn't Aunt Polly that Mr. Pendleton loved long ago, and so we aren't going there to live. I told you it was but I made a mistake. I hope you didn't tell anyone," she finished anxiously.

"No, I didn't tell anyone, Pollyanna," replied the doctor, a little queerly.

"That's all right then." Pollyanna sighed in relief. "You see you're the only one I told, and I thought Mr. Pendleton looked sort of funny when I said I'd told you."

"Did he?" The doctor's lips twitched.

"Yes. And of course he wouldn't want many people to know it — when it wasn't true. But why don't you get a woman's hand and heart, Dr. Chilton?"

There was a moment's silence, then the doctor said, "They're not always to be had for the asking, Pollyanna."

"But I should think you could get 'em," Pollyanna argued.

"Thank you," replied the doctor, "but I'm afraid some of your older sisters would not agree."

Pollyanna frowned again. Then her eyes widened in surprise.

"Dr. Chilton, you don't mean you tried to get somebody's hand and heart once, like Mr. Pendleton, and — "

The doctor got to his feet abruptly.

"Never mind about that now, Pollyanna. Suppose you run back now to Mrs. Snow. I've written down the name of the medicine and how she is to take it. Was there anything else?"

Pollyanna shook her head.

"No sir, thank you, sir," she murmured, as she turned toward the door. From the hallway she called back, "Anyhow, I'm glad it wasn't my mother's hand and heart that you wanted, Dr. Chilton. Good-by!"

It was on the last day of October that the

accident occurred. Pollyanna, hurrying home from school, crossed the road — apparently at a safe distance — in front of a swiftly approaching motor car.

Just what happened, no one could tell afterward. Neither was there anyone who could tell why it happened or who was to blame that it did happen. But at five o'clock Pollyanna was borne, limp and unconscious, into the little room that was so dear to her. She was undressed tenderly and put to bed by a white-faced Aunt Polly and a weeping Nancy. Dr. Warren, hastily summoned by telephone, was hurrying as fast as another motor car could bring him from the village.

Nancy was sobbing to Old Tom in the garden after the doctor had arrived and was closeted in the hushed room.

"Is she hurt bad?" The old man's voice shook.

"There ain't no telling," sobbed Nancy. "She lay back that white an' still she might easy be dead. But Miss Polly said she wasn't dead — an' Miss Polly ought to know if anyone would, she kept up such a listening an' a feeling for her heartbeats an' her breath."

"But where is she hurt?"

"I don't know, I don't know," moaned Nancy. "There's a little cut on her head, but 'tain't bad, Miss Polly says. She says she's afraid it's infernally she's hurt."

"I guess you mean internally, Nancy," Old Tom said. "She's hurt infernally, all right — plague take that automobile!"

"I don't know, I don't know," moaned Nancy, with a shake of her head as she turned away. "Seems as if I just can't stand it till that doctor gets out of there. I wish I had a washing to do — the biggest washing I ever see," she wailed, wringing her hands helplessly.

Even after the doctor was gone, however, there seemed to be little that Nancy could tell Mr. Tom. There appeared to be no broken bones, and the cut was of slight consequence. But the doctor had looked very grave. He had shaken his head slowly, and had said that time alone could tell. After he had gone, Miss Polly looked even paler and more drawn than before. The patient had not recovered consciousness, but at present she seemed to be resting as comfortably as could be expected. A trained nurse had been sent for and would come that night. That was all. Nancy turned away sobbing and went back to her kitchen.

It was sometime during the next forenoon that Pollyanna opened her eyes and realized where she was.

"Why, Aunt Polly, what's the matter? I can't get up," she moaned, falling back on the pillow, after trying to lift herself.

"No dear, I wouldn't try just yet," said her aunt quickly, but very quietly.

"But what's the matter? Why can't I get up?"

Miss Polly's eyes asked an agonized question of the white-capped young woman standing in the window out of range of Pollyanna's eyes.

The young woman nodded.

"Tell her," the lips said.

Miss Polly cleared her throat and tried to swallow the lump that would scarcely let her speak.

"You were hurt, dear, by the automobile last night. But never mind that now. Aunty wants you to rest and go to sleep again."

"Oh, yes. I — I ran." Pollyanna's eyes were dazed. She lifted her hand to her forehead. "Why it's done up, and it hurts!"

"Yes, dear, but never mind. Just — just rest."

"But Aunt Polly, I feel so funny, and so bad! My legs feel so queer — only they don't feel at all!"

With an imploring look into the nurse's face, Miss Polly struggled to her feet and turned away. The nurse came forward quickly.

"Suppose you let me talk to you now," she began cheerily. "It's high time we were getting acquainted. I am Miss Hunt, and I've come to help your aunt take care of you. And the very first thing I'm going to do is ask you to swallow these little white pills for me."

Pollyanna's eyes grew a bit wild.

"But I don't want to be taken care of. I want to get up. I go to school, you know. Can't I go to school tomorrow?"

From the window where Aunt Polly stood, came a half-stifled cry.

"Tomorrow?" replied the nurse brightly. "Well, I may not let you out quite so soon as that, Miss Pollyanna. But just swallow these pills for me, and we'll see what they'll do."

"All right," Pollyanna agreed, somewhat doubtfully. "But I must go to school the day after tomorrow — there are examinations then."

She spoke again, a minute later. She spoke of school and of the automobile and of how her head ached. But very soon her voice trailed into silence under the blessed influence of the medicine she had swallowed.

John Pendleton

POLLYANNA DID NOT GO to school the next day, or the day after. Pollyanna, however, did not realize this. She did not realize anything very clearly until a week had passed. Then the fever subsided, the pain lessened somewhat, and her mind awoke to full consciousness. Then she had to be told all over again what had occurred.

"So I'm hurt and not sick," she said at last. "Well, I'm glad of that."

"Glad, Pollyanna?" asked her aunt, who was sitting by the bed.

"Yes. I'd so much rather have broken legs like Mr. Pendleton than be a life-long invalid like Mrs. Snow. Broken legs get well."

Miss Polly, who had said nothing whatever about broken legs, got to her feet and walked to the little dressing table across the room. She was picking up one object after another, and putting each down in an aimless fashion quite unlike her usual decisiveness. Her face was not aimless-looking at all, however. It was white and drawn.

On the bed Pollyanna lay blinking at the dancing band of colors on the ceiling, which came from one of the prisms in the window.

"I'm glad it isn't smallpox that ails me too," she murmured. "That would be worse than freckles. And I'm glad it isn't whooping cough — I've had that, and it's horrid — and I'm glad it isn't appendicitis or measles, 'cause they're catching — measles are, I mean — and they wouldn't let you stay here."

"You seem to be glad for a good many things, my dear." Aunt Polly put her hand to her throat as if her collar bound.

Pollyanna laughed softly.

"I am. I've been thinking of 'em all the time I've been looking at that rainbow. I love rainbows. I'm so glad Mr. Pendleton gave me those prisms! I'm glad of some things I haven't said yet. I'm almost glad I was hurt."

"Pollyanna!"

Pollyanna laughed softly again. She turned luminous eyes on her aunt. "Well, you see, since I've been hurt you've called me dear lots of times — and you didn't before. I love to be called dear — by someone who belongs to me. Some of the Ladies' Aiders did call me that, and of course that was pretty nice, but you belong to me. Oh, Aunt Polly, I'm so glad you belong to me!"

Aunt Polly did not answer. Her eyes were full of tears. She had turned away and was hurrying from the room.

It was that afternoon that Nancy ran out to Old Tom, who was cleaning harnesses in the barn. Her eyes were wild.

"Mr. Tom, guess what's happened," she panted. "You couldn't guess in a thousand years!"

"Then I won't try," retorted the old man, grimly, "specially as I probably ain't got more'n ten to live, anyhow. You'd better tell me, Nancy."

"Well, listen then. Who do you suppose is in the parlor now with the mistress? Who?"

Old Tom shook his head.

"It's John Pendleton!"

"You're joking, girl."

"Not much I am — and me a-letting him

173

in myself — crutches an' all! Just think, Mr. Tom — *him* a-calling on *her!*"

"Well, why not?" demanded the old man.

Nancy gave him a scornful glance.

"As if you didn't know!" she derided.

"Eh?"

"Oh, you needn't be so innocent," she retorted with mock indignation, " — you what led me wild-goose chasing in the first place!"

"What do ye mean?"

Nancy glanced through the open barn door toward the house and came a step nearer to the old man.

"Listen! It was you that was telling me about Miss Polly in the first place, wasn't it? Well, one day I thinks I finds two and two, and I puts 'em together and makes four. But it turns out to be five — and no four at all, at all!"

"If you're goin' to talk to me, you've got to talk plain horse sense," Old Tom declared testily. "I never was no hand for figures."

Nancy laughed.

"Well, it's this," she explained. "I heard somethin' that made me think he was Miss Polly's feller."

"*Mr. Pendleton!*" Old Tom straightened up.

"Yes. Oh, I know now he wasn't. It was Pollyanna's mother he was in love with and that's why he wanted — but never mind that part." She remembered just in time her promise to Pollyanna not to tell that Mr. Pendleton had wanted her to come and live with him. "Well, I've been asking folk about him, and I've found out that him and Miss Polly ain't been friends for years. She's been hating him like poison owing to the silly gossip that coupled their names together when she was eighteen or twenty."

"Yes, I remember." Old Tom nodded. "It was three or four years after Miss Jennie went off with the other chap. Miss Polly knew about it, of course, and was sorry for him, so she tried to be nice to him. Maybe she overdid it a little — she hated that minister chap so who took away her sister. At any rate, somebody begun to make trouble. They said she was running after him."

"Running after any man — *her!*" interjected Nancy.

"I know it, but they did," declared Old Tom. "And of course no gal of any spunk'll stand that. Then about that time come the trouble with her own feller. After that she shut up like an oyster and wouldn't have nothin' to do with nobody. Her heart just seemed to turn bitter at the core."

"Yes, I know. I've heard about that," replied Nancy. "And that's why you coulda knocked me down with a feather when I see him at the door — him, what she ain't spoke to for years! But I let him in and went and told her."

"What did she say?" Old Tom held his breath.

"Nothing — at first. She was so still I thought she hadn't heard, and I was just going to say it over when she speaks up quiet like: 'Tell Mr. Pendleton I will be down at once.' I told him, then I come out here and told you," finished Nancy, casting another backward glance toward the house.

"Humph!" grunted Old Tom, and fell to work again.

In the parlor of the Harrington homestead, Mr. John Pendleton did not have to wait long before a swift step warned him of Miss Polly's coming. As he attempted to rise, she made a gesture of protest. She did not offer her hand, however, and her face was coldly reserved.

"I called to ask about Pollyanna," he began at once, a little brusquely.

"Thank you. She is about the same," said Miss Polly.

"And that is? Won't you tell me *how* she is?" His voice was not quite steady this time.

A quick spasm of pain crossed Miss Polly's face.

"I can't. I wish I could!"

"You mean you don't know?"

"Yes."

"But the doctor?"

"Dr. Warren himself seems at sea. He is in correspondence now with a New York specialist. They have arranged for a consultation."

"But what were her injuries? That you do know?"

"A slight cut on the head, one or two bruises, and an injury to the spine which seems to have caused paralysis from the hips down.

A low moan came from the man. There was a brief silence, then he said:

"And Pollyanna — how does she take it?"

"She doesn't understand how things really are. And I can't tell her."

"But she must know something!"

"Oh, yes. She knows she can't move, but she thinks her legs are broken. She says she's glad it's broken legs like yours because broken legs get well. She talks like that all the time, until it seems as if I should die!"

Through the blur of tears in his own eyes, the man saw the drawn face opposite, twisted with emotion. His thoughts went back to what Pollyanna had said, "Oh, I couldn't leave Aunt Polly — now!"

It was this thought that made him ask very gently, "I wonder if you know, Miss Harrington, how hard I tried to get Pollyanna to come and live with me."

"With you! — Pollyanna!"

The man winced a little at the tone of her voice, but his voice was impersonally cool when he spoke again.

"Yes. I wanted to adopt her — legally, you understand, making her my heir of course."

The woman in the opposite chair relaxed a little. It came to her, suddenly, what a brilliant future it would have meant for Pollyanna — this adoption. She wondered if Pollyanna were old enough and mercenary enough to be tempted by this man's money and position.

"I am very fond of Pollyanna," Mr. Pendleton continued. "I am fond of her both for her own sake, and for her mother's. I stood ready to give Pollyanna the love that had been twenty-five years in storage."

"*Love!*" Miss Polly remembered suddenly why she had taken this child in the first place, and with the recollection came the remembrance of Pollyanna's own words uttered that very morning. "I love to be called dear by folks that belong to me!" It was this love-hungry little girl who had been offered the stored-up affection of twenty-five years. With a sinking heart Miss Polly realized that. With a sinking heart she realized something else, too: the dreariness of her own future without Pollyanna.

"Well?" she said. And the man, recognizing the self-control that vibrated through the harshness of the tone, smiled sadly.

"She would not come," he answered.

"Why?"

"She would not leave you. She said you had been so good to her. She wanted to stay with you — and she said she thought you wanted her to stay," he finished, as he pulled himself to his feet.

He did not look toward Miss Polly. He turned his face resolutely toward the door. But instantly he heard a swift step at his side and found a shaking hand thrust toward him.

"When the specialist comes and I know anything definite about Pollyanna, I will let you hear from me," Miss Polly said in a trembling voice. "Good-by and thank you for coming. Pollyanna will be pleased."

On the day after John Pendleton's call at the Harrington homestead, Miss Polly set herself to the task of preparing Pollyanna for the visit of the specialist.

"Pollyanna, my dear," she began gently,

179

"we have decided that we want another doctor besides Dr. Warren to see you."

"Dr. Chilton! Oh, Aunt Polly," Pollyanna interrupted, "I'd so love to have Dr. Chilton! I've wanted him all the time, but I was afraid you didn't. But I'm so glad you do want him!"

Aunt Polly's face had turned white, then red, then back to white again. But when she answered, she showed very plainly that she was trying to speak lightly and cheerfully.

"Oh, no dear! It wasn't Dr. Chilton at all that I meant. It is a new doctor — a very famous doctor from New York who knows a great deal about hurts like yours."

Pollyanna's face fell.

"I don't believe he knows half so much as Dr. Chilton."

"Oh, yes, he does. I'm sure, dear."

"But it was Dr. Chilton who doctored Mr. Pendleton's broken leg, Aunt Polly. If you don't mind very much, I would like to have Dr. Chilton — truly I would!"

For a moment Aunt Polly did not speak at all, then she said gently, yet with a touch of her old stern decisiveness:

"But I do mind, Pollyanna. I mind very much. For reasons which I do not care to speak of now, I don't wish Dr. Chilton called in on this case."

Pollyanna still looked unconvinced.

"But, Aunt Polly, if you loved Dr. Chilton — "

"What, Pollyanna?" Aunt Polly's voice was very sharp now. Her cheeks were very red too.

"I say, if you loved Dr. Chilton, and didn't love the other one," sighed Pollyanna, "seems to me that would make some difference in the good he would do — and I love Dr. Chilton."

The nurse entered the room at that moment and Aunt Polly rose to her feet abruptly, a look of relief on her face.

"I am very sorry, Pollyanna," she said, a little stiffly, "but I'm afraid you'll have to let me be the judge this time. Besides, it's already arranged. The New York doctor is coming tomorrow."

As it happened, however, the New York doctor did not come the next day owing to his sudden illness. This led Pollyanna into a renewed pleading for the substitution of Dr. Chilton.

But as before, Aunt Polly shook her head and said "no, dear" very decisively, yet with an anxious assurance that she would do anything but that to please Pollyanna.

A Door Ajar

Just a week from the time Dr. Mead, the specialist, was first expected, he came. He was a tall, broad-shouldered man with kind gray eyes and a cheerful smile. Pollyanna liked him at once and told him so.

"You look quite a lot like my doctor," she added.

"Your doctor?" Dr. Mead glanced in evident surprise at Dr. Warren, talking with the nurse a few feet away. Dr. Warren was a small, brown-eyed man with a pointed brown beard.

"Oh, that isn't my doctor," explained Pollyanna. "Dr. Warren is Aunt Polly's doctor. My doctor is Dr. Chilton."

"Oh-h!" said Dr. Mead, his eyes resting on Miss Polly, who had turned hastily away.

Pollyanna hesitated, then continued with her usual truthfulness. "You see, I wanted Dr. Chilton, but Aunt Polly wanted you. She said you knew more than Dr. Chilton about broken legs like mine. And of course if you do, I can be glad for that. Do you?"

"Only time can tell that, little girl," the doctor said gently, then turned a grave face toward Dr. Warren, who had just come to the bedside.

Everyone said afterward that it was the cat that did it. Certainly, if Fluffy had not poked his nose and paw against Pollyanna's unlatched door, the door would not have swung noiselessly open on its hinges. And if the door had not been open, Pollyanna would not have heard her aunt's words.

Miss Polly, the two doctors, and the nurse stood talking in the hall. In Pollyanna's room, Fluffy had just jumped to the bed when Aunt Polly's agonized exclamation sounded clearly and sharply through the open door.

"Not that! Doctor, not that! You don't mean the child will *never walk* again!"

It was all confusion then. From the bedroom came Pollyanna's terrified "Aunt Polly

— Aunt Polly!" Then Miss Polly, seeing the open door and realizing that her words had been heard, gave a low moan and for the first time in her life fainted dead away.

The nurse, with a choking, "She heard!" stumbled toward the open door. The two doctors stayed with Miss Polly.

"Miss Hunt, please, I want Aunt Polly. I want her right away, please!"

The nurse closed the door and came forward hurriedly. Her face was very pale.

"She can't come just this minute, dear. She will — a little later. What is it? Can't I get it?"

Pollyanna shook her head.

"I want Aunt Polly — she said something. I want her to tell me it isn't true — it isn't true!"

The nurse tried to speak, but no words came. Something in her face sent an added terror to Pollyanna's eyes.

"Miss Hunt, you heard her! It *is* true! Oh, it *isn't* true! You don't mean I can't ever walk again?"

"There, there, dear — don't, don't!" choked the nurse. "Perhaps he didn't know. Perhaps he was mistaken. There's lots of things that could happen, you know."

"But Aunt Polly said he did know!"

"Yes, yes, I know, dear. Just — just don't think anymore about it now — please don't dear."

Pollyanna flung out her arms wildly.

"But I can't help thinking about it," she sobbed. "It's all there is now to think about."

"There, there, dear, just take this," Miss Hunt said. "Things aren't half as bad as they seem, dear, lots of times, you know."

Obediently Pollyanna took the medicine, and sipped the water from the glass in Miss Hunt's hand.

"I know. That sounds like things Father used to say." Pollyanna faltered, blinking off the tears. "He said there was always something about everything that might be worse, but I reckon he never just heard he couldn't walk again. I don't see how there can be anything that could be worse — do you?"

Miss Hunt did not reply. She could not trust herself to speak just then.

Two Visits

Nancy was sent to tell Mr. Pendleton of
Dr. Mead's verdict. There had been a time
when Nancy would have rejoiced at this extraordinary opportunity to see something of
the House of Mystery and its master. But today her heart was too heavy to rejoice at anything. She scarcely even looked about her
during the few minutes she waited for John
Pendleton to appear.

"I'm Nancy, sir," she said respectfully, in
response to the surprised questioning of his
eyes, when he came into the room. "Miss Harrington sent me to tell you about Miss Pollyanna."

"Well?"

"It ain't well, Mr. Pendleton," she choked.

"You don't mean — " He paused, and she bowed her head miserably.

"Yes, sir. He says — she can't walk again — never."

For a moment there was absolute silence in the room; then the man spoke in a voice shaking with emotion.

"Poor little girl! Poor little girl!"

Nancy glanced at him, but dropped her eyes at once. She had not supposed that sour, cross, stern John Pendleton could look like that.

"She herself doesn't know yet of course, does she?"

"But she does, sir," sobbed Nancy, "and that's what makes it all the harder. She found out — drat that cat! I begs yer pardon," apologized the girl, hurriedly. "It's only that the cat pushed open the door and Miss Pollyanna overheard 'em talking. She found out that way."

"Poor little girl!" said the man again.

"Yes, sir. You'd say so sir, if you could see her," choked Nancy. "I ain't seen her but twice since she knew about it, and it done me up both times. You see it's all so fresh and new to her, and she keeps thinking all the time of new things she can't do now. It wor-

ries her, too, 'cause she can't seem to be glad
— maybe you don't know about her game,
though," broke off Nancy apologetically.

"The glad game?" asked the man. "Oh yes,
she told me of that."

"Oh she did! I guess she told it generally to
most folks. But you see, now she can't play it
herself, and it worries her. She says she can't
think of a thing about this not walking again
to be glad about."

"Well, why should she?" retorted the man,
almost savagely.

Nancy shifted her feet uneasily.

"That's the way I felt too, till I happened
to think — it would be easier if she could find
something, you know. So I tried to remind
her."

"To remind her of what?" John Pendleton's
voice was still impatient.

"Of — of how she told others to play it, and
what she said for them to do."

Nancy paused, but the man did not speak.
He sat with his hand over his eyes.

"Then I tried to remind her how she used to
say the game was all the nicer to play when
— when it was hard," resumed Nancy, in a
dull voice. "But she says that too is different
— when it really *is* hard. I must be going now,
sir," she broke off abruptly.

At the door she hesitated, turned, and asked timidly: "I couldn't be telling Miss Pollyanna that you'd seen Jimmy Bean again, I suppose, sir, could I?"

"I don't see how you could as I haven't seen him," observed the man a little shortly. "Why?"

"Nothing, sir, only — well, you see, that's one of the things that she was feeling bad about — that she couldn't take him to see you. She said she'd taken him once, but she didn't think he showed off very well that day. She was wanting to take him again, she said, so's to show you he really was a lovely child's presence. Maybe you know what she means by that, sir. Drat that automobile! I begs yer pardon, sir. Good-by!" And Nancy fled precipitately.

It did not take long for the entire town of Beldingsville to learn that the great New York doctor had said Pollyanna Whittier would never walk again. Never before had the town been so stirred. Everybody knew the piquant little freckled face by sight and almost everybody knew of the "game."

In kitchens and sitting rooms, and over backyard fences women talked of it and wept openly. On street corners and in store lounging places the men talked too, and wept, though not so openly.

Almost at once, the mistress of the Harrington homestead greatly to her surprise began to receive callers: people she knew, and people she did not know — men, women, and children — many of whom Miss Polly had not supposed that her niece knew at all.

Some came in and sat down for a stiff five or ten minutes. Some stood awkwardly on the porch steps. Some brought a book, a bunch of flowers, or a dainty to tempt the palate. Some cried openly. Some turned their backs and blew their noses furiously. But all inquired very anxiously for the little injured girl, and all sent her some message — and it was these messages which, after a time, stirred Miss Polly to action.

First came Mr. John Pendleton.

"I don't need to tell you how shocked I am," he began almost harshly. "But can nothing be done?"

Miss Polly gave a gesture of despair.

"Dr. Mead prescribed certain treatments and medicines that might help, and Dr. Warren is carrying them out to the letter, of course. But Dr. Mead held out almost no hope."

John Pendleton rose abruptly, though he

had just come. His face was white, and his mouth was set into stern lines. At the door he turned.

"I have a message for Pollyanna," he said. "Will you tell her, please, that I have seen Jimmy Bean and that he's going to be my boy hereafter. Tell her I thought she would be — glad to know. I shall adopt him, probably."

For a brief moment Miss Polly lost her usual well-bred self-control.

"You will adopt Jimmy Bean?" she gasped.

"Yes. I think Pollyanna will understand. You will tell her I thought she would be — glad?"

"Why, of — of course," faltered Miss Polly.

"Thank you." John Pendleton bowed as he turned to go.

In the middle of the floor Miss Polly stood, silent and amazed, still looking after the man who had just left her. John Pendleton *adopt* Jimmy Bean? John Pendleton, wealthy, independent, morose, reputed to be miserly, and supremely selfish, to adopt a little boy — and such a little boy?

With a somewhat dazed face Miss Polly went upstairs to Pollyanna's room.

"Pollyanna, I have a message for you from Mr. John Pendleton. He has just been here. He says to tell you he has taken Jimmy Bean for his little boy. He said he thought you'd be glad to know it."

Pollyanna's face flamed into sudden joy.

"Glad? Glad? Well, I reckon I am glad! Oh, Aunt Polly, I've so wanted to find a place for Jimmy — and that's such a lovely place! Besides I'm so glad for Mr. Pendleton too. Now he'll have the child's presence."

"The — what?"

Pollyanna colored painfully. She had forgotten that she had never told her aunt of Mr. Pendleton's desire to adopt her.

"The child's presence," stammered Pollyanna, hastily. "Mr. Pendleton told me once, you see, that only a woman's hand and heart or a child's presence could make a home. And now he's got it — the child's presence."

"Oh, I see," said Miss Polly very gently. And she did see — more than Pollyanna realized. She saw something of the pressure that was probably brought to bear on Pollyanna herself at the time John Pendleton was asking her to be his child's presence and transform his great pile of gray stone into a home. "I see," she finished, her eyes stinging with sudden tears.

Pollyanna, fearful that her aunt might ask further embarrassing questions, hastened to lead the conversation away from the Pendleton house and its master.

"Dr. Chilton says so too — that it takes a woman's hand and heart or a child's presence to make a home," she remarked.

Miss Polly turned with a start.

"Dr. Chilton! How do you know — that?"

"He told me so. When he said he lived in just rooms — not a home."

Miss Polly did not answer. She was looking out the window.

"So I asked him why he didn't get 'em — a woman's hand and heart — and have a home."

"Pollyanna!" Miss Polly had turned sharply. Her cheeks showed a sudden color.

"Well, I did. He looked so sorrowful."

"What did he — say?" Miss Polly asked the question as if some force within her was urging her not to ask it.

"He didn't say anything for a minute, then he said very low that you couldn't always get 'em for the asking."

There was a brief silence. Miss Polly's eyes had turned again to the window. Her cheeks were still unnaturally pink.

Pollyanna sighed.

"He wants one, anyhow, I know, and I wish he could have one."

"Pollyanna, how do you know?"

"Because afterwards, on another day, he said something else. He said that low too, but I heard him. He said that he'd give all the world if he did have one woman's hand and heart. Why, Aunt Polly, what's the matter?" Aunt Polly had risen and hurriedly gone to the window.

"Nothing dear. I was changing the position of this prism," said Aunt Polly, whose whole face was now aflame.

The Game and Its Players

IT WAS NOT LONG after John Pendleton's second visit that Milly Snow called one afternoon. Milly Snow had never before been to the Harrington homestead. She blushed and looked very embarrassed when Miss Polly entered the room.

"I — I came to inquire for the little girl," she stammered.

"You are very kind. She is about the same. How is your mother?" asked Miss Polly.

"That is what I came to tell you — that is, to ask you to tell Miss Pollyanna," said Milly breathlessly and incoherently. "We think it's — so awful — so perfectly awful that the little thing can't ever walk again, and after all she's done for us — for Mother, you know, teaching her to play the game, and all that. When we remembered all the things she'd said to us, we thought if she could only know what she had done for us, that it would help, you know, in her own case, about the game, because she could be glad — that is, a little glad — " Milly stopped helplessly, and seemed to be waiting for Miss Polly to speak.

Miss Polly had sat politely listening, but only about half of what had been said had she understood. She was thinking now that she always had known that Milly Snow was strange but she had not supposed she was crazy. When a pause came she filled it with a quiet:

"I don't think I quite understand, Milly. Just what is it that you want me to tell my niece?"

"Yes, that's it. I want you to tell her," answered the girl feverishly. "Make her see what's she's done for us. Of course she's seen some things, because she's been there, and she knows Mother is different. But I want her to know how different she is — and me too. I'm different. I've been trying to play it — the game — a little."

Miss Polly frowned. She would have asked what Milly meant by the game, but there was no opportunity. Milly was rushing on again with nervous volubility.

"You know nothing was ever right before — for Mother. But now she lets me keep the shades up, and she takes interest in things — how she looks, and all that. And she's actually begun to knit little things — bibs and baby blankets for fairs and hospitals. And she's so interested and so glad to think she can do it! That was all Miss Pollyanna's doing, you know. You can't think what a different room it is now, what with the red and blue and yellow worsteds. And the prisms in the window that she gave her — why it actually makes you feel better just to go in there now. Before I used to dread it awfully. It was so dark and gloomy, and Mother was so unhappy you know.

"So we want you to please tell Miss Pollyanna that we understand it's all because of her. That we thought, maybe if she knew it, it would make her a little glad that she knew us. And — and that's all," sighed Milly, rising hurriedly to her feet. "You'll tell her?"

"Why, of course," murmured Miss Polly, wondering how much of this remarkable discourse she could remember to tell.

These visits of John Pendleton and Milly Snow were only the first of many; and always there were the messages — the messages which were in some ways so curious that they caused Miss Polly more and more to puzzle over them.

One day there was the little Widow Benton. Miss Polly knew her well, though they had never called upon each other. She knew her as the saddest little woman in town — one who always was in black. Today, however, Mrs. Benton wore a knot of pale blue at her throat, though there were tears in her eyes. She spoke of her grief and horror at the accident; then she asked diffidently if she might see Polly-anna.

Miss Polly shook her head.

"I am sorry, but she sees no one yet. A little later, perhaps."

Mrs. Benton wiped her eyes, rose, and turned to go. But after she had almost reached the hall door she came back hurriedly.

"Miss Harrington, perhaps you'd give her a message," she stammered.

"Certainly, Mrs. Benton. I shall be very glad to."

Still the little woman hesitated, then she spoke.

"Will you tell her, please, that — that I've put on this," she said, touching the blue bow at her throat. "She's been trying for so long to make me wear some color, that I thought she'd be glad to know I'd begun." Mrs. Benton shook her head and turned away. "If you'll just tell Pollyanna — she'll understand." And the door closed after her.

A little later that same day there was the other widow — at least she wore widow's garments. Miss Polly did not know her at all.

She wondered vaguely how Pollyanna could have known her. The lady gave her name as "Mrs. Tarbell."

"I'm a stranger to you, of course," she began at once. "But I'm not a stranger to your niece. I've been at the hotel all summer long, and every day I've had to take long walks for my health. It was on these walks that I met your niece — she's such a dear little girl! I wish I could make you understand what she's been to me. I was very sad when I came up here, and her bright face and cheery ways reminded me of my own little girl, that I lost years ago. I was so shocked to hear of the accident, and then when I heard that the poor child would never walk again, I just had to come to you."

"You are very kind," murmured Miss Polly.

"I — I want you to give her a message from me. Will you?"

"Certainly."

"Will you just tell her that Mrs. Tarbell is glad now. Yes, I know it sounds odd, and you don't understand, but, if you'll pardon me, I'd rather not explain." Sad lines came to the lady's mouth, and the smile left her eyes. "Your niece will know just what I mean, and I felt that I must tell her. Thank you and pardon me, please, for any seeming rudeness in my call," she said, as she took her leave.

Thoroughly mystified now, Miss Polly hurried upstairs to Pollyanna's room.

"Pollyanna do you know a Mrs. Tarbell?"

"Oh, yes. She's sick and awfully sad. She stays at the hotel and takes long walks. We go together. I mean we used to." Pollyanna's voice broke, and two big tears rolled down her cheeks.

Miss Polly cleared her throat hurriedly.

"Well, she's just been here, dear. She left a message for you — but she wouldn't tell me what it meant. She said to tell you that Mrs. Tarbell is glad now."

"Did she say that — really?" Pollyanna clapped her hands softly. "Oh, I'm so glad!"

"But Pollyanna, what did she mean?"

"Why, it's the game, and — " Pollyanna stopped short.

"What game?"

"Nothing much, Aunt Polly, that is — I can't tell it unless I tell other things that I'm not to speak of."

It was on Miss Polly's tongue to question her niece further, but the obvious distress on Pollyanna's face stayed the words before they were uttered.

Not long after Mrs. Tarbell's visit, the climax came. It came in the shape of a call from a certain young woman with unnaturally pink cheeks and abnormally yellow hair — a young woman who wore high heels and cheap jewelry; a young woman whom Miss Polly knew very well by reputation, but whom she was angrily amazed to meet beneath the roof of the Harrington homestead.

Miss Polly did not offer her hand. She drew back, indeed, as she entered the room.

The woman rose at once. Her eyes were very red, as if she had been crying. Half defiantly she asked if she might, for a moment, see the little girl, Pollyanna.

Miss Polly said no. She began to say it very sternly, but something in the woman's eyes made her add the civil explanation that no one was allowed to see Pollyanna yet.

The woman hesitated, then a little brusquely she spoke. Her chin was still at a slightly defiant tilt.

"My name is Mrs. Payson — Mrs. Tom Payson. I presume you've heard of me — most of the good people in town have — and maybe some of the things you've heard ain't true. But never mind that. It's about the little girl I came. I heard about the accident, and it broke me all up. Last week I heard how she couldn't ever walk again, and — and — "

She paused and cleared her throat, but

when she resumed her voice was still husky.

"Maybe you don't know it, but I've seen a good deal of that little girl of yours. We live on the Pendleton Hill road, and she used to go by often — only she didn't always go by. She came in and played with the kids and talked to me — and my man, when he was home. She seemed to like us. She didn't know, I suspect, that her kind of folks don't generally call on my kind. Maybe if they did call more, Miss Harrington, there wouldn't be so many of my kind," she added, with sudden bitterness.

"Be that as it may, she came, and she didn't do herself no harm, and she did do us good — a lot of good. How much she won't know — nor can't know.

"But it's just this. It's been hard times with us this year, in more ways then one. We've been blue and discouraged — my man and me — and ready for most anything. We was reckoning on getting a divorce and letting the kids — well, we didn't know what we would do with the kids. Then came the accident, and what we heard about the little girl's never walking again. We got to thinking how she used to come and sit on our doorstep and play with the kids and laugh and just be glad. She was always being glad about something and then one day she told us about the game, and tried to coax us to play it.

"Well, that's what I came to tell her today — that maybe she can be a little glad for us, 'cause we've decided to stick to each other, and play the game ourselves. I knew she would be glad, because she used to feel kind of bad at things we said sometimes. Just how the game is going to help us, I can't say that I exactly see yet, but maybe it will. Anyhow, we're going to try — 'cause she wanted us to. Will you tell her?"

"Yes, I will tell her," promised Miss Polly, a little faintly. Then, with sudden impulse, she stepped forward and held out her hand. "And thank you for coming, Mrs. Payson," she said.

The defiant chin fell. The lips above it trembled visibly. Mrs. Payson clutched at the outstretched hand, turned, and fled.

The door had scarcely closed behind her before Miss Polly was confronting Nancy in the kitchen.

"Nancy!"

Miss Polly spoke sharply. Not since Miss Pollyanna's accident had Nancy heard her mistress speak so sternly.

"Nancy, will you tell me what this absurd game is that the whole town seems to be babbling about? And what, please, has my niece to do with it? Why does everybody from Milly Snow to Mrs. Tom Payson send word to her that they're playing it? As near as I can judge, half the town are putting on blue ribbons or stopping family quarrels or learning to like something they never liked before, and all because of Pollyanna. I tried to ask the child herself about it, but I can't seem to make much headway, and of course I don't like to worry her — now. Can you tell me what it all means?"

To Miss Polly's surprise and dismay, Nancy burst into tears.

"It means that ever since last June that blessed child has been making the whole town glad, and now they're turning around and trying to make her a little glad too."

"Glad of what?"

"Just glad! That's the game."

Miss Polly actually stamped her foot.

"There you go like all the rest, Nancy. What game?"

Nancy lifted her chin. She faced her mistress and looked her squarely in the eye.

"I'll tell ye, ma'am. It's a game Miss Pollyanna's father learned her to play. She got a pair of crutches once in a missionary barrel when she was wanting a doll, and she cried, of course, like any child would. Then her father told her that there wasn't anything but what there was something about it that you could be glad about, and that she could be glad about them crutches."

"Glad for crutches!" Miss Polly choked back a sob — she was thinking of the helpless little girl on the bed upstairs.

"Yes'm. That's what I said, and Miss Polly-anna said that's what she said too. But he told her she could be glad — 'cause she didn't need 'em."

"Oh-h!" cried Miss Polly.

"And after that she said he made a regular game of it — finding something in everything to be glad about. They called it the just being glad game. That's the game, ma'am. She's played it ever since."

"But how — how — " Miss Polly came to a helpless pause.

"She's made me glad on such a lot of things — little things and big things — and it's made 'em so much easier," Nancy maintained. "For instance, there's Monday mornings that I used to hate so. She's actually made me glad for Monday mornings."

"Glad — for Monday mornings!"

"I know it does sound nutty, ma'am." Nancy laughed. "But let me tell you. I hated Monday mornings something awful, and what does Pollyanna up and tell me one day but this: 'Well, Nancy, I should think you could be gladder on Monday morning than any other day in the week, because it would be a whole week before you'd have another one!' I'm blest if I ain't thought of it every Monday morning since — and it *has* helped, ma'am. It made me laugh, anyhow, every time I thought of it. And laughing helps you know."

"But why hasn't she told me the game?" faltered Miss Polly. "Why did she make such a mystery of it when I asked her?"

Nancy hesitated.

"Begging yer pardon, ma'am, you told her not to speak of her father, so she couldn't tell you. It was her father's game, you see."

Miss Polly bit her lip.

"She wanted to tell you, first off," continued Nancy, a little unsteadily. "She wanted somebody to play it with, you know. That's why I begun it — so she could have someone."

"Well, I know somebody who'll play it now," choked Miss Polly, as she turned and sped through the kitchen doorway.

Behind her, Nancy stood staring amazedly.

"Well, I'll believe anything now," she muttered to herself.

A little later, in Pollyanna's room, the nurse left Miss Polly and Pollyanna alone together.

"And you've had another caller today, my dear," announced Miss Polly, in a voice she vainly tried to steady. "Do you remember Mrs. Payson?"

"Mrs. Payson? I reckon I do! She lives on the way to Mr. Pendleton's. She's got the prettiest little baby girl three years old, and a boy almost five. She's awfully nice and so's her husband — only they don't seem to know how nice each other is. Sometimes they fight — I mean they don't quite agree. They're poor too, they say, and of course they don't ever have barrels, 'cause he isn't a missionary minister, like — well he isn't.

"But she wears real pretty clothes, sometimes, in spite of their being so poor," resumed Pollyanna in some haste. "She says she's going to get a divorce. What is a divorce, Aunt Polly? I'm afraid it isn't very nice, because she didn't look happy when she talked about it. And she said if she did get it, they wouldn't live there anymore and that Mr. Payson would go away, and maybe the children too."

"But they aren't going away my dear," said Aunt Polly. "They're going to stay right there together."

"Oh, I'm so glad! Then they'll be there when I go up to see — Oh dear!" broke off the little girl, miserably.

"There, there, don't," choked her aunt. "Perhaps you'll drive up sometime. But listen! I haven't told you, yet, all that Mrs. Payson said. She wanted me to tell you that they were going to stay together and play the game, just as you wanted them to."

"Did they, really? Oh, I am glad of that!"

"Yes, she said she hoped you'd be. That's why she told you — to make you glad, Pollyanna."

Pollyanna looked up quickly.

"Why, Aunt Polly, you spoke just as if you knew. Do you know about the game, Aunt Polly?"

"Yes, dear." Miss Polly forced her voice to be cheerfully matter-of-fact. "Nancy told me. I think it's a beautiful game. I'm going to play it now — with you."

"Oh, Aunt Polly — you? I'm so glad? You see, I really wanted you most of anybody, all the time."

Aunt Polly caught her breath a little sharply. It was even harder this time to keep her voice steady, but she did it.

"Yes, dear. Why, Pollyanna, I think all the town is playing that game with you now — and the whole town is happier."

"Oh, I'm so glad," Pollyanna cried. Then suddenly a wonderful light illumined her face. "Aunt Polly, there is something I can be glad about, after all. I can be glad I had my legs — else I couldn't have done that!"

Through an Open Window

Oɴᴇ ʙʏ oɴᴇ the short winter days came and went — but they were not short to Pollyanna. They were long and sometimes full of pain. Very resolutely, however, Pollyanna was turning a cheerful face toward whatever came.

She saw people now, occasionally, and always there were the messages from those she could not see. They brought her something new to think about — and Pollyanna needed new things to think about.

The winter passed, and spring came. There seemed every reason to believe that Dr. Mead's worst fears would be realized — that Pollyanna would never walk again.

Beldingsville, of course, kept itself informed concerning Pollyanna, and in Beldingsville, one man in particular fumed and fretted himself into a fever of anxiety over Pollyanna's condition. As the days passed, however, and the news came to be no better, something besides anxiety began to show in the man's face — despair and a dogged determination. It was then that Mr. John Pendleton, somewhat to his surprise, received a Saturday morning visit from Dr. Thomas Chilton.

"Pendleton," began the doctor, abruptly, "I've come to you because you, better than anyone else in town, know something of my relationship with Miss Polly Harrington."

John Pendleton started visibly — he did know something of the situation between Polly Harrington and Thomas Chilton, but the doctor had not mentioned the matter for fifteen years or more.

"Yes," Pendleton said, trying to make his voice sound concerned enough for sympathy, and not eager enough for curiosity.

"Pendleton, I want to see that child. I want to make an examination. I *must* make an examination."

"Well can't you?"

"Can't I! Pendleton, you know very well I haven't been inside that door for more than fifteen years. The mistress of that house told me that the next time she asked me to enter it, I might take it that she was begging my pardon, and that things would be as before — which meant that she'd marry me. Perhaps you see her summoning me now — but I don't!"

"But couldn't you go — without a summons?"

"Well, hardly. I have some pride, you know."

"But if you're so anxious — couldn't you swallow your pride and forget the quarrel —"

"Forget the quarrel!" interrupted the doctor, savagely. "I'm not talking of that kind of pride. So far as that is concerned, I'd go there on my knees — or on my head — if that would do any good. It's professional pride I'm talking about. It's a case of sickness, and I'm a doctor. I can't butt in and say, 'Here take me!' — can I?"

"Chilton, what was the quarrel?" asked Pendleton.

The doctor made an impatient gesture, and got to his feet.

"What was it? What's any lovers' quarrel — after it's over?" he said, pacing the room angrily. "So far as I am concerned I am willing to say there was no quarrel. Pendleton, I must see that child. It may mean life or death. I honestly believe it will mean — nine chances out of ten — that Pollyanna Whittier will walk again!"

The words were spoken clearly, and they were spoken just as the doctor reached the open window near John Pendleton's chair. Thus it happened that they reached the ears of the young boy kneeling beneath the window on the ground outside.

Jimmy Bean, at his Saturday morning task of pulling up weeds in the flowerbeds, sat up with ears and eyes wide open.

John Pendleton was asking "What do you mean?"

"I mean that from what I can hear and learn — a mile from her bedside — that her case is very much like that a college friend of mine has just helped. For years he's been making this sort of thing a special study. I've kept in touch with him and studied too, and from what I hear — but I want to *see* the girl!"

"You must see her, man!" John Pendleton urged. "Couldn't you — say, through Dr. Warren?"

The other shook his head.

"I'm afraid not. Warren has been very decent though. He told me himself that he suggested consultation with me, but Miss Harrington said no so decisively that he didn't dare venture it again. But, Pendleton, I've got to see Pollyanna. Think of what it may mean to her if I do!"

"Yes, and think of what it will mean if you don't!" retorted Pendleton.

"But how can I, without a direct request from her aunt — which I'll never get!"

"She must be made to ask you."

"How?"

"I don't know."

"She's too proud and too angry to ask me. But when I think of that child, doomed to life-long misery, and when I think that maybe in my hands lies a chance of escape —" He did not finish his sentence, but with his hands thrust deep into his pockets he turned and began to stomp up and down the room again.

"But if she could be made to see — to understand," urged John Pendleton.

"Who's going to do it?" demanded the doctor.

"I don't know, I don't know," groaned the other miserably.

Outside the window Jimmy Bean suddenly stirred. Up to now he had scarcely breathed, so intently had he listened to every word.

"Well, by Jinks, I know!" he whispered. "*I'm* a-goin' to do it!" He rose to his feet, crept stealthily around the corner of the house, and ran with all his might down Pendleton Hill.

Jimmy Takes the Helm

"It's Jimmy Bean. He wants to see you, ma'am," announced Nancy in the doorway.

"Me?" asked Miss Polly, plainly surprised. "Are you sure he did not mean Miss Pollyanna?"

"Yes'm. He said it was you he wanted."

"Very well, I'll come down." Miss Polly rose from her chair a little wearily.

In the sitting room she found Jimmy Bean waiting for her, and he began to speak at once.

"Ma'am, I suppose it's dreadful what I'm doing, an' what I'm saying but I can't help it. It's for Pollyanna, and I'd walk over hot coals for her. I think you would too, if you thought

there was a chance for her to walk again. An'
so that's why I come to tell you that as long
as it's only pride that's keeping Pollyanna
from walking, why I knew you would ask Dr.
Chilton here if you understood — "

"Wh-at?" interrupted Miss Polly, the look
of stupefaction on her face changing to one of
angry indignation.

Jimmy sighed despairingly.

"There, I didn't mean to make you mad.
That's why I begun by telling you about her
walking again. I thought you'd listen to that."

"Jimmy, what are you talking about?"

"I'm tryin' to tell you."

"Well, then tell me. But begin at the beginning, and be sure I understand each thing as
you go."

Jimmy wet his lips determinedly.

"Well, to begin with, Dr. Chilton came to
see Mr. Pendleton, and they talked in the library. Do you understand that?"

"Yes, Jimmy." Miss Polly's voice was rather
faint.

"Well, the window was open, and I was
weeding the flowerbed under it, and I heard
'em talk."

"Oh, Jimmy! Listening?"

" 'Twasn't about me, an' 'twasn't sneak listening," bridled Jimmy. "And I'm glad I lis-

tened. You will be when I tell you. Why, it may make Pollyanna walk!"

"Jimmy, what do you mean?" Miss Polly was leaning forward eagerly.

"Well, Dr. Chilton knows some doctor somewhere that can cure Pollyanna, he thinks — but he can't tell till he sees her. And he told Mr. Pendleton that you wouldn't let him."

Miss Polly's face turned very red.

"But, Jimmy, I — I can't — I couldn't! That is I didn't know!" Miss Polly was twisting her fingers together helplessly.

"Yes, and that's what I come to tell you, so you would know," asserted Jimmy, eagerly. "I heard that for some reason — I didn't rightly catch what — you wouldn't let Dr. Chilton come, and you told Dr. Warren so. Dr. Chilton couldn't come himself, without you asked him, on account of pride an' professional et- et- well, et- something, anyway. They was wishing somebody could make you understand, only they didn't know who could. I was outside the window, an' I says to myself, 'By Jinks, I'll do it!' An' I come — an' have I made you understand?"

"Yes. But, Jimmy, about that doctor?" asked Miss Polly. "Who was he? What did he do? Are they *sure* he could make Pollyanna walk?"

"I don't know who he was. They didn't say. Dr. Chilton knows him, and he just cured somebody just like her, Dr. Chilton thinks. You will let him come, won't you? — now you understand?"

Miss Polly turned her head from side to side. Her breath was coming in little uneven gasps. Jimmy, watching her with anxious eyes, thought she was going to cry. But she did not cry. After a minute she said brokenly:

"Yes — I'll let — Dr. Chilton — see her. Now run home, Jimmy, quick! I've got to speak to Dr. Warren."

The next time Dr. Warren entered Pollyanna's room a tall broad-shouldered man followed close behind him.

"Dr. Chilton! Oh, Dr. Chilton, how glad I am to see you!" cried Pollyanna. "Oh, then you asked him to come," murmured Pollyanna to her aunt.

"Yes, dear, I asked him. That is — " But it was too late. The happiness that had leaped to Dr. Chilton's eyes was unmistakable and Miss Polly had seen it. With very pink cheeks she turned and left the room hurriedly.

Over in the window the nurse and Dr. Warren were talking earnestly. Dr. Chilton held out both his hands to Pollyanna.

"One of the very gladdest jobs you ever did has been done today, Pollyanna," he said in a voice shaken with emotion.

At twilight a wonderfully different Aunt Polly came to Pollyanna's bedside. The nurse was at supper. They had the room to themselves.

"Pollyanna, dear. Oh, Pollyanna, I'm so happy! And so glad, darling!"

"Aunt Polly, were *you* the woman's hand and heart Dr. Chilton wanted so long ago? You were — I know you were! And that's what he meant by saying I'd done the gladdest job of all today. I'm so glad, Aunt Polly!"

"Perhaps, some day, dear — " But Aunt Polly did not finish. She did not dare tell Pollyanna the great hope that Dr. Chilton had put into her heart. But she did say this — and surely this was quite wonderful enough to Pollyanna's mind:

"Pollyanna, next week you're going to take a journey. You're going to a great doctor who has a hospital many miles from here. He's a dear friend of Dr. Chilton's and we're going to see what he can do for you!"

A Letter from Pollyanna

"DEAR AUNT POLLY AND UNCLE TOM: I can — I can — I *can* walk! I did today all the way from my bed to the window! It was six steps. My, how good it was to be on legs again!

"All the doctors stood around and smiled, and all the nurses stood beside them and cried. I don't see why they cried. *I* wanted to sing and shout and yell! Just think, I can walk — walk — walk! Now I don't mind being here, and I didn't miss the wedding anyhow. Wasn't that just like you, Aunt Polly, to come here and get married so I could see you.

"Pretty soon, they say, I shall go home. I wish I could walk all the way there. I don't think I shall ever want to ride anywhere any more. It will be so good just to walk. Oh, I'm so glad! I'm glad for everything. I'm going to walk eight steps tomorrow.

"With heaps of love to everybody,

"POLLYANNA"

THE END